The Little Book
of

Short Stories
&
True

by

Award-Winning Author

Carrie King

For

Rebekah, Zoë, Hannah,

Paige, Elle, Beth

and

Louie

Cover Photography by © Rebekah French

'A view of Lake Geneva, Switzerland'

March 2015

Photograph of Carrie King by **Trevor Leighton**
Holder of the largest number of photographs on display by a single photographer in
The National Portrait Gallery in **London.**

Copyright © Carrie King 2015

ISBN: 978 - 0 - 9932227 - 1 - 9

Published by Bothy Books

Printed in the United Kingdom

2 4 6 8 10 9 7 5 3 1

Acknowledgements

Huge thanks to **all** the people, especially **Jean Downs** and **Lily Clark**, who have encouraged (and nagged), me to compile these stories, alongside a few personal poems and a little essay.

Thank you to the superb photographer, **Trevor Leighton,** for taking the shot of my face and making me look half-decent!

A massive thank you to Journalist, **Pam Francis**, who is my Mentor of long ago and still continues to cheer me on in the work I love!

Special thanks to **Rebekah French**, who is a really creative photographer and shot the wonderful photograph for the cover of this little book, by Lake Geneva in Switzerland.

A special thank you to **Roger** and **Julie Chant** for letting me write in their lovely place in L'Orée du Bois, France.

Many thanks to **all** the people with whom I have enjoyed the real-life events included in these short stories.

Grateful thanks to **www.visit-dorset.com** for allowing me to include two of their beautiful images of Lyme Regis

I greatly appreciate **Martin Dubrovsky** for letting me use his absolutely stunning photograph of 'Camping in Le Dramont'.

Many, many, many thanks to my Doctor, **Melanie Munro**, who has always supported me through my darkest (and lightest), hours!

Words of Appreciation

"**The Little Book of Short Stories & True** is a wonderful 'can't put it down' book. Every story is captivating and some will bring a tear to your eye."
Valerie London

"A lovely little book. '**My Glenys**' took me back to my childhood and more simple times. The book was a joy for me to read!" **Janice Schaub**

"I loved Carrie King's stories: they are full of romance, twists and surprises!"
Kathleen Kelynack

"Compelling reading. Carrie King takes us on a journey of beautifully written and thought-provoking short stories that capture us from the very beginning. Highly recommended!" **Karen Davison (Author)**

" 'The Face' is one great poem!"
Jeff Fleischer (Poet)

"**The Little Book of Short Stories & True** includes: adventure, a hint of romance and unexpected twists, which makes for compelling reading: 5 out of 5 stars. HIGHLY recommended!"
Janelle Davies (Artist and Illustrator)

"Carrie King shares part of herself in **The Little Book of Short Stories & True**. I enjoyed reading it so much!"
Sue Turner

"I loved '**The Ticket**' it was a compelling, endearing & moving read."
Jane Durnford

"I feel honoured to have read and shared Carrie King's writings in **The Little Book of Short Stories & True**. I have been left with impressions of warm summers and blue seas." **Moira Davies**

"Carrie King's stories are full of intrigue: so many times I ask, 'Where is this one going?' Her work is so romantic with delicate and different surprises. The book is really well written and the verse is so fascinating, I like to read it over and over. I look forward in anticipation to Carrie's next compilation of Short Stories: I can't wait!" **Kathy Young**

"Lyrical prose and heartfelt stories come together perfectly to give a glimpse into the author's heart!" **Michael Joseph**

"I am not a keen reader but **The Little Book of Short Stories & True** soon changed all that. Once I picked it up, I couldn't put it down! Carrie King has such an incredible talent for capturing memories and reflections of life that we, as readers, feel as though we are actually there, in the moment, experiencing it: such a joy to read!" **Nia Budding**

"Each story captures your attention and draws you in. I feel as if I'm reading in a beautiful, peaceful garden on a spring day. The stories involve you in a variety of emotional responses and, true to life, illustrate the dark and light (and all the shades in between), of every person's life. The inclusion of some of Carrie's poetry works so well. It truly is a very engaging book!" **Brenda Dyson**

"Your book is a reflection of time that has stood still but has a hope for the future. Your best friend, always." **Lily Clark (Author)**

"A little Treasure Trove of short stories and poems." **Sylvia Ellis**

"It's like a little insight into Carrie's heart. I love it!" **Lesley Alvarado**

A Note from the Author

All of these short stories are based around true events. All bar one (Anne's Farewell), include events that have been either in my life or have a family connection to my life. All but one were entered into Short Story, Flash Fiction or Micro Fiction Competitions, which made me limited to a specific number of words in every case (such a strain but good for me, a writer who always says, 'Why use one word when you can use ten').

A poet I am not, but I do love observing everything around me, especially when I travel and I do so love describing that, which I see, in rhyming prose and using plenty of alliteration!

I hope you enjoy reading them as much as I have enjoyed writing them.

Carrie King

26th May 2015

P.S. As this is a revised edition, I am so happy that a few of the many amazing comments sent in from you Readers have been included! Thank you so much, everyone of you who reads this little book of mine! C.K.

Table of Contents

Photographs

Photographs (continued)

1

The Ticket

Minnie stumbled nervously, fumbling in her cloth purse, desperately trying to locate it.

"It's here…..I know it is," she apologized, delving deeper and peering into the darkness of the tapestry bag.

The man behind the desk grunted impatiently, looking past Minnie and down the long line of people, queuing restlessly, behind her.

She hadn't wanted to emigrate; it was all James' idea.

"Canada is the place to be, Min," he had enthused. "I can't believe I've landed such a topping position. Head of English in Vancouver's most prestigious school? What more could we want?"

'To stay in England,' Minnie had thought to herself, 'to be near Mama. Every girl needs her mother at this time.'

Filled with optimism, James had sailed to Canada ahead of Minnie and keenly awaited her arrival.

The man behind the desk tapped his thin fingers thunderously against the polished wood and cleared his throat ready to speak, when another official looking man marched up to Minnie.

"Would you step this way please, Madam?" he asked, guiding Minnie's arm and escorting her into his office.

Minnie just stood there looking lost, anxious and bemused.

"I……I……do……have……a……ticket," she stammered, trying, yet

again, to extricate it.

"I am quite sure you do, otherwise you most certainly wouldn't have stood, waiting for hours to board, in that infernal queue!"

"What's wrong?"

"Er…..there's a problem…...with your condition," said the man, casting his eye, very briefly, down Minnie's very rounded front.

Minnie had hardly dared tell James. It's not that they hadn't wanted children but a baby, within ten months of being married, was not something they had planned. However, James embraced this new circumstance with all the gusto and excitement that Minnie had come to expect of him.

"We just don't have the facilities onboard, it's as simple as that," said the man. "If something went wrong, there would be nowhere to take you and no-one to take care of you. You are…..er…..too…..er….. heavy with…..er…..child; consequently, we are refusing your right of passage."

Minnie stood silently. What was there to say? She would not be joining James in Canada: as the man said, it was 'as simple as that'. Amidst the mixture of emotions, however; the relief of not having to cross the massive Ocean alone and the joy of returning back to Mama, Minnie detected a disappointment lurking. Did the thought of a new, exciting life beckon? No matter: her pregnant state had forced the issue and so, after the man had directed Minnie to the Telegraph Office, she had hastily sent James a brief message and then found herself in a Hackney Carriage, searching for some cheap lodgings in Southampton, to sit and wait.

James couldn't believe it when he opened his newspaper! How could this be? Suddenly, all of his hopes and dreams, his plans for his beloved Minnie and their child, his delight in this newfound life in Canada, went surging from him. He sobbed and groaned piteously.

The next day the dreaded telegram arrived. James put it on the mantelpiece and left it unopened.

A colleague arrived to visit his newly-made friend. Poor, hapless James had not eaten, shaved nor changed his clothes for three days.

"James, you look awful, you smell and why on earth haven't you opened your telegram?"

"Huh, and why......to read of my wife's and baby's cruel demise?"

His friend opened the telegram and chortled, thrusting the small piece of white paper under James' nose.

"You Priceless Twerp!"

James read the words, 'Refused passage on Titanic STOP Waiting in Southampton STOP Hurry little money STOP Minnie STOP'.

James returned to England and taught in a little country school. Josephine Rachel, their daughter, my mother, was born in early August 1912......

.....and the Ticket?

It is still a treasured item in my family, to this very day.

THE END

NOTE: As we all know, it was 100 years from the sinking of **RMS Titanic** in April 2012. Sadly, since I was a very late baby, I never knew any of my four grandparents, including Minnie. My Mother, Josephine Rachel, Minnie's baby, always used to say to me that if Minnie had boarded **The Titanic**, then she undoubtedly would have died and so would my, then unborn, mother, as Minnie's ticket was in

Steerage and most of these passengers were trapped behind locked gates on that fateful night and went down with the ship.

Obviously Minnie being turned away from **The Titanic** is very, very significant in our family, as none of us would have been born had Minnie been allowed to board, so, thank you, White Star Officials!

Carrie King

Here is a photograph of me with Minnie's baby, Josephine Rachel, my mother, who was born in August 1912. My mother died several years ago: this was taken a few days before she died.

Minnie, my beautiful Grandmother, who was refused passage on the Titanic (I only saw her for the first time last year and I cried)!

Josephine, Minnie's baby, my Mother, who was also refused passage on The Titanic!

2

Saint-Georges-de-Didonne

(I wrote this on a paper receipt while I was sitting in a restaurant overlooking the beach in Sainte-Georges-de-Didonne, France. The three 'horses' I saw were simply three fishing cranes out to sea that resembled horses).

Long beach of sand,

Footprints.

Cream cliffs so grand,

Sea glints.

Long arms and hands,

Volley ball.

Castles in sands,

Turrets tall.

White crests unfurled,

Foaming.

Dogs wet and curled,

Roaming.

Men, French and tanned,

Sailing.

Sea birds on land,

Wailing.

Kites full and fine,

Soaring.

Bread, cheese and wine,

Pouring.

Sky meets the cranes,

Three horses.

Café des Bains,

Four courses.

3

'The Girl from Ipanema'

The Girl from Ipanema
(English Lyrics by Norman Gimbel)

'Tall and tanned and young and lovely
The girl from Ipanema goes walking
And when she passes, each one she passes
Goes "A-a-a-h".
When she walks she's like a samba
That swings so cool and sways so gentle
That when she passes, each one she passes
Goes, "A-a-a-h".
Oh, but I watch her so sadly.
How can I tell her I love her?
Yes, I would give my heart gladly
But each day as she walks to the sea,
She looks straight ahead, not at me.
Tall and tanned and young and lovely
The girl from Ipanema goes walking
And when she passes, I smile, but she
Doesn't see, she just doesn't see.'

I have often wondered what became of him. I have often wondered what became of her. I have often thought of him and occasionally I have thought of her. Sometimes, when peering into the ledger of my life, I have read to a handful of faithful friends, the few pages that tell the tale of how they both, briefly, touched my time.

Although many years have passed and once-important events that should have been remembered may have long fled my mind, a few inconsequential instances have stayed, luminous and marked in my heart and head, never to be erased. My memory of that brief summer occurrence has not dimmed in the tiniest.

There is something everlasting that youth brings us; something that never leaves us. Although our faces might change, our bodies might weaken and our memories might fail us in many matters, nothing can, nor will, stop us from remembering the exuberance of being young: the excitement, the joy, the wonder of discovery, the agony of love tangled amidst the sheer bliss of living.

France has always excited me. From the moment I first stepped off the Boat Train in Dieppe, there began a wondrous love affair with this diverse country and Her people. Although English is the language of my heart, hearing French spoken thrilled me. Watching the busyness of everyone bustling about enthralled me. Observing the interaction of passers-by fascinated me and of course, the smell of freshly baked bread and newly brewed coffee intoxicated me.

It appeared each person I spied had their own special mission. Take just two, for instance:-

The Widow: how sadly she would walk along, clad in black from toe to top, carrying her deep, wicker basket, heavily laden with fresh fruit and vegetables and sprouting golden baguettes she had just bought from the marché du matin. Whilst her panier à provisions straddled one arm, she would lift up the other, only to pull her black, silk headscarf tightly down over her bushy, dyed, burgundy hair. Her body appeared weary from grief and mourning but her legs seemed to purposefully carry her onwards and homewards; perhaps that was down to the prospect of her forthcoming breakfast or maybe it was merely the thought of her daily visit to the early morning market soon being over and dispensed with for yet another day. With her nose to her shoes, she would stop for no-one, she would speak to no-one; her face, as made of white lead, looked blank and bereft of feeling.

The Road Sweeper: how decisively he would sweep the square-cobbled streets, bordered by tall, terraced houses and shops that stood straight on to the paths that were cluttered with shutters and lined with lamp posts. With his large, wide, stiff broom, he would stroke away at the previous day's discarded Gauloises packets flung amidst endless cigarette butts, empty wine bottles, random pages of yesterday's news and fragments of leftover food that even the roaming dogs had found unpalatable. Frequently, his day would be interrupted by passing friends, acquaintances and strangers. Always smiling, he would stop his work to shake hands and exchange a few pleasantries or amusing anecdotes with them. Then on he would go with short, rhythmic strokes, brushing his streets like a Parisian painter, which, alas, he was not, as the buildings along his narrow lanes always looked so forlorn and abandoned and desperately in need of a new coat of paint. His face would glow, however, when his job was done for the day and his last road had been swept clean.

Appropriately, it was in this much beloved Country that spoke a language of Romance, that I first encountered them. She was the one I noticed first and when I saw her, the old, famous song, '**The Girl from Ipanema**', came leaking into my mind, soaking my thoughts. She was, undeniably, '**Tall and tanned and young and lovely'.** All the staff and students on our International Field Trip, in Saint Raphaël, Southern France, noticed her. One couldn't help but do so; blessed with flawless features, she was exquisite.

'**The girl from Ipanema goes walking**,' the lyrics of the song continue: and walk she did, although, I think 'glide' might be a more appropriate verb. She had this amazing way of moving. Apart from her astounding legs, the boundaries of which beggared belief, nothing else stirred. Her entire, faultless torso remained static, almost as if in suspended animation.

'**And when she passes, each one she passes goes "A-a-a-h".**' Indeed they did, especially me. I hope I am not one to be prone to jealousy, envy or covetousness but I yearned to look as she did. I longed to be so tall and tanned and lovely. (The 'young' part was indisputable)!

Tall? Sadly, I had not been blessed with such a stature that could possibly be referred to as 'tall'. I was five feet, six inches in height; pretty much falling into the 'average' category I imagine; not tall, at all.

Tanned? Hmmmm…..I was fair skinned (ish), which meant my skin did not automatically deepen into a natural looking tan when exposed to the sun's merciless rays, as '**The girl from Ipanema's**' did. Freckle, yes, but it took days of gentle warming before my skin transformed into a light golden glow.

Lovely? Je ne sais pas.

'**But each day as she walks to the sea, she looks straight ahead, not at me.**' These words, too, rang so true. I longed for her to see me but, of course, she didn't. She was a tower of inaccessibility, aloof and remote, a fortress against intruders. Her eyes would never deem to glance below her, to those beneath her in every way. She simply floated past us, not even aware that others might be there. How I wanted to be like that citadel of seclusion, that bastion of privacy. Not a chance; I was open, laughed too loud and too often and always at the most inappropriate times.

'**And when she passes, I smile but she doesn't see. She just doesn't see.**' And when she passed, I smiled but, immediately, I felt foolish, stupid even, to think that one so admired might lower herself to smile back at me. She did not see me or anyone else; in fact, not once did I see her smile.

'What about her boyfriend then?' You might well ask. He was a perfect complement to her: beautiful in every way. Tall and tanned, too, with an immaculate, muscular, toned body, sun-bleached blond hair and the darkest brown eyes that melted and moulded every female, regardless of age or size, into a nubile woman of extraordinary allure. All of us girls, the female Tutors too, drooled over him, sending us into a mumbling, incoherent stupor each time he passed. I reaped great pleasure from surreptitiously spying on him, as he was always smiling and stopping to talk to anyone and everyone, from child to old man. He truly appeared the antithesis of Her. Both members of this eye-catching couple were part of the Dutch Student Group, working and camping alongside us.

Each day, fatigued from a few of hours of largely, uninspiring Field Work, we would rush down to the blue pebbled beach of Le Dramont to savour the remaining afternoon sunshine. The sea before us wasn't simply any sea. No, this was The Mediterranean. The climate was always warm and pleasant and the distinctive, deep, blue water was renowned for its most agreeable temperature. No hesitation was necessary to wade or plunge straight in, as it felt as delightful as a warm, relaxing bath. Having no tides, no waves, no folds to hamper the strokes of anyone's style, little exertion was needed to swim in this Maritime Haven on the sunny Cote d'Azur. I had to enjoy soaking in this salty sea, all by myself, though, as my friends preferred stone-baking on the sunny shore.

About a mile off the coast lay a small island, which really intrigued me. Hungry for exploration, I invited my fellow students to swim out to it. "No!" their expected response boomed around the beach. Knowing all efforts to stop me answering any call of adventure would be futile, they looked on as I set off, entirely alone, stroking determinedly through the glassy sea. They continued lazing under the blazing sun: on reflection, is it any wonder I came a shade or three lower in the 'Tanning Ratings'?

It was here, whilst swimming alone to this island that I first encountered Him without Her. I had enjoyed the challenge of reaching this red rock via a leisurely swim but when I arrived I was met with bitter disappointment as there were copious notices declaring that the island was 'Private Property' and no one unauthorised was allowed to land or trespass. (Later I learned it was called Île d'Or, had a Medieval Tower built on the russet rocks and inspired Hergé's book, 'The Black Island', in the famous **Tintin** Series).

Made famous or not, I was frustrated with this discovery and circled all around the rocks until I found a small, sheltered cove where I could simply enjoy floating and reflecting on the amazing clarity of the azure sea.

For a while, soothed by the silence and serenity, I lay on top of the smooth, still water with the sun on my outstretched body. This blissful tranquillity was then arrested by an odd lapping noise coming from under an overhanging ledge. Curious as to the source of this strange sound, I was just about to investigate when a gangling, male swimmer came splashing noisily around the corner, gate-crashing my private Sea Party. I was unimpressed when this uninvited guest stopped swimming un-comfortably near me, forcing me to stop floating, drop my legs vertically and start treading water. I was asked, in French, if it had taken long for me to swim to the island. Not given a moment to reply, I was dutifully

Île d'Or where I lay on the sea

informed that I was one of the English Group! I was not granted even the tiniest of slots to comment, so it was then relayed to me that his visit to London was both planned and imminent. My unwanted visitor then droned on, delivering dull details of dreary events, scarcely stopping for breath. I kept thinking, 'At the third stroke it will be three-thirty-three and thirty-three seconds precisely'. I imagined this talkative French fellow as a clockwork man, complete with a huge, fixed key on his back, ready for anyone to wind up, apart from me, that is. Unworthy thoughts, perhaps but it was extremely obvious that my being classed as 'in' this conversation was totally erroneous: the only part I played was a non-speaking one, albeit a constantly-smiling one.

It was while the Speaking Clock whirred on that I was startled by a second swimmer whose very blond head emerged from the ledge, under which I had heard the lapping sounds. To my surprise, the unmistakable, heart-stopping, brown eyes of our Dutch Obsession looked straight into mine as they passed by me on one side, while he executed a near-perfect, front crawl. I shook, which was ludicrous as no word, no sound, no tiny utterance even, had passed between us. I was mortified that He had been so nearby and apparently without '**The girl from Ipanema**' in tow and yet I hadn't been aware of it!

Very quickly, I excused myself from the Clockwork Man and swam off, eager to get back to my friends. I breathlessly related to them how I had been in such close proximity to Him. All the girls giggled with excitement. Of course, there was nothing to tell, no answers to give to their barrage of questions, as the meeting had been but a fleeting moment. Nevertheless, they kept surmising what 'might' have happened, had the Frenchman not turned up. This was exceedingly absurd as nothing would have happened, He hadn't even noticed me.

Le Dramont's blue, pebbled beach with Île d'Or out to sea

That evening, whilst at dinner, I was told by my friends that apparently, I had been the topic of conversation among the male French Students, in their shower room. The eager swimmer had told tall tales of how we had 'got to know each other'. Considering the only words that fell out of my mouth were, "Excusez-moi, je dois aller," they must have been very tall indeed!

For the next few days, He and '**The girl from Ipanema**' continued walking around on display and we all continued to sigh as they passed us by.

The week eventually drew to a close and a Beach Party was arranged for us to enjoy our last night together in France. A feast of barbequed French sausages was laid on for us, accompanied by a tasty range of cheeses, juicy white grapes and hunks of luscious, hot, French bread: most delicious, especially washed down with a glass of superb Sancerre, fermented and produced from the celebrated Sauvignon Blanc grape, planted in the sprawling vineyards of the Loire Valley. Hmmmm.......

We sang and we danced. I am not particularly talented at much, but dancing? Well, I can do that with or without talent and Boogie I did. It was fun and invigorating. After hours of non-stop laughing and bopping, I walked along the beach away from the masses and found a secluded circle of craggy boulders, where I was sure no-one would find me. I simply needed a bit of space, some quiet time. I clambered through a gap in this ring of rocks, folded my cardigan, which was always tied unnecessarily around my waist, into a shape of sorts and lay on the dry, smooth sand, resting my head on my makeshift cushion. I looked up at the marvellous, star-filled night sky. After the noisy music, it was a joy to hear nothing but the sound of the gentle breeze caressing the surface of the sea. Intoxicated by the beauty of it all, my eyes closed in pleasure, like a nursing cat suckling her kittens. This was bliss.

'Nothing', I thought, 'nothing, irrefutably, could possibly beat this.'

Only a few seconds into this delight, however, I heard footsteps and I became aware of a figure looking over one of the rocks of my private shelter. I couldn't make out who it was as they stood in the shadows. I dreaded it was the Speaking Clock, determined to bombard me, once more, with some mechanised monologue. Deftly, the figure climbed up and over the top of a rock, jumped down and landed very close to me in my secret, sandy room.

"Do you mind if I join you?" asked this beautiful, male voice in perfect English with just a hint of an unknown accent. Unquestionably, this was not a clockwork man. The owner of the very attractive voice then, to my surprise, proceeded to lie down beside me. He uttered no words for a few minutes, which greatly unnerved me. I, too, stayed silent.

"Do you know how long I have been trying to get an opportunity to speak with you....alone, to be with you.....alone?"

I continued in my unspoken state, not quite grasping exactly that, which was happening. The worst of it was that I hadn't the courage to turn and look to see who it was that expressed these extraordinarily ridiculous things.

"Hmmmm....." he said, "I see you have a comfortable pillow for your head. I don't have one. Do you mind if I use your lovely pillows to rest my head?"

I turned my head exceedingly rapidly towards him, affronted by his audacity, only to be greeted by His gorgeous smile!

His identity should not have swayed me from my instant desire to chastise such insolence but as I looked into his yearning, brown eyes looking down into mine, I dissolved into some form of unusual, human jelly fish.

"So? May I then?" He asked, looking first at me and then at the rounded objects of his request.

I didn't reply: so, taking this silence as consent, he proceeded to lay his handsome head gently on my chest.

I didn't know what to do. I was a moral girl, untouched and pure but somehow his appeal seemed neither dishonourable nor objectionable. In fact, it gave me great pleasure. So much so, that, trembling, I lifted up one of my arms and ran my hand through his thick, sun-streaked locks. How delectable it was to feel his hair running smoothly through my fingers!

"Hmmmmm......" He murmured. "That feels good; you have such a gentle touch."

Still, not a single word had left my lips.

"You are so different from all the other girls," He whispered, gazing up at me, "you always seem to be having fun: you are always smiling and laughing. I love it! Do you know how appealing that is? I looked at you dancing all evening; you dance as if there is nobody else about."

He then, gently, stroked my face and said softly, "You have such a beautiful face."

'Did he say he looked at me dancing all evening? Did he say I had a beautiful face?' I mused, shaking my head.

"Stop shaking your head, you know it's true!" He laughed, pulling himself up so his face was really close to mine. He smelt wonderful and feeling his breath on my cheeks as he spoke stirred unimaginable feelings from deep down inside me. "I have thought about you all week. From the moment I first saw you, I have wanted to do this ...."

With these words, he covered my mouth with his and thus began a breathtaking night of indescribably, incredible kissing (no wonder I am still a great advocate of this wonderfully expressive act). Bear in mind that this occurred several decades ago, when most girls still presented themselves at the altar in their maiden state and that included me.

During those beautiful hours, he would sometimes stop and tell me how soft and sensuous I was and how much he wanted to spend time with me; how he just had to see me again. He told me how he even followed me out to sea when I swam to the island, hoping that he would get a chance of talking to me alone. He said he momentarily lost courage when he reached the isle and hid under an overhanging ledge but that wasn't so bad, as it afforded him the pleasurable opportunity of observing me as I lay floating in the sun, looking so happy and free. He made me laugh when he said how annoyed he was that 'some blundering Frenchman' arrived and started talking to me. He said he was really jealous!

Was I in a dream? Was he really talking about me? His hungry kisses, that even to this very moment, I remember so vividly, told me he was but still I doubted that I was capable of arousing such a magnificent example of Manhood to such heights!

Oh, what a night (sounds like a song I love)! Every moment was spent kissing, talking and laughing. We finally walked back to my tent at five in the morning, still kissing, talking and laughing. I whispered I had to go and he pulled me back into him and kissed me some more. Eventually, reluctantly, I left him and entered the tent of sleeping students.

'Camping in Le Dramont'

by kind permission of Martin Dubrovsky
((This is exactly how I remember the campsite in Le Dramont)).

I was far, far too excited to sleep. I just lay on my bed and went over in my mind, every beautiful detail of that unbelievable night. Then it suddenly occurred to me that he hadn't even mentioned '**The girl from Ipanema**' and neither had I and I felt terribly guilty.

The next morning we were summoned to see the Dutch Students off. I was dreading it! My Mother had always told me never to kiss on a first date or boys wouldn't respect me and here was I, knowing He and I hadn't even had a date and yet we had kissed passionately for hours and, worse still, He was very evidently in a committed relationship, not free for me, at all.

Herded into a long line facing the Dutch Bus, we stood ready to wave off our fellow workers with a hearty farewell. I waited anxiously for the fearful moment when '**The girl from Ipanema**' and her boyfriend would appear.

It happened exactly as I knew it would. Her arm tightly linked in his, both walked past me and '**He looked straight ahead, not at me**'. '**And when He passes, I smile but He doesn't see. He just doesn't see.**' My mother was right. I stood there amidst the throng, feeling cast aside like yesterday's rubbish.

How thankful I was I hadn't breathed a word to any of my friends. I knew then the night before had been a wonderful experience that only I would ever know about; no-one would have believed me, anyway!

I tried not to show any emotion but I couldn't help myself; I was a wounded bird but fortunately, not fatally, so my little head lifted itself up and did what it did best, its face smiled and laughed with the other students: although too long and too raucously. I pretended I didn't care, I just didn't care. I glanced fleetingly towards the happy couple and in the corner of my eye, I watched them both climb up the steps into the Carriage that was to take my Prince away forever. Yes, Cinderella did go to the Ball but this time she was not to live happily ever after. They walked along almost to the back of the bus and sat down, with the Goddess of Aloofness sitting by the window. I couldn't bear to look at Him.

The French Students then turned up, including the Speaking Clock. He made a bee-line for me and I let him get rather close; I even allowed him to put his arm around my waist. How mean was I? I fobbed off a friend, when she asked if I was all right. She said she could clearly see tears welling up in my eyes. I told her it was simply the wind and blocked tear ducts. (I ask you)? Brilliant explanation, especially as there wasn't the slightest breeze that day.

As I continued laughing nervously and far too noisily, someone said very loudly,

"Hello, what's he up to now? What has he forgotten?"

A hush fell over the crowd as He stood up and walked along the entire length of the coach and got off. He walked straight up to me, pushing the Clockwork Man to one side and, taking me in his beautiful, strong, tanned arms, gave me a long, lingering kiss. Everyone gasped really loudly. When this luscious task was over, he handed me an envelope.

"Here are all my details: full name, address and telephone number. Make sure you contact me......please?" His brown eyes entreated.

He then kissed me again and walked back on to the bus, this time sitting close to the front. He smiled and blew me kisses right up until the bus had chugged away and was out of sight.

I never did write or telephone Him; as much as I wanted to, as much as I yearned to.

"Why ever not?" You may ask.

The answer to that is quite simple.

I never could, nor cannot still, even after such a long time, get out of my head, '**The girl from Ipanema's**' face, staring at me through the glass window of the coach. As I looked at it, gone was the proud, inaccessible look: the aloofness had completely vanished. Now she appeared as a widow, in mourning, totally grief stricken; her face was as made of white lead, looking blank and bereft of feeling.

As for Him: well, he was smiling, his face was glowing and he looked every bit as if his job had been successfully completed for that day. His face said it all; he was definitely ready to start a new day as his last road had been swept clean.

THE END

4

Rosa's Lesson

(Micro Fiction)

They were not a typical sight, walking along with us in our little, sleepy, English Town. Our African guests were both over six feet tall and draped in their magnificent ceremonial dress of finest, hand-woven Kente; the vibrant, Ghanaian cloth of many colours. Their lavish regalia and gold jewelry truly portrayed them as they indeed were, distinguished members of the Royal Ashanti Court. Their beautiful black faces shone like ebony in the early evening sun.

As we arrived for their Official Reception at The Town Hall, our close Italian friends' four-year-old little girl, Rosa, came bounding up, beside herself with joy. I picked her up and kissed her on her red, rosy cheek and she kissed me back on my pale white face. She stroked my head and said,

"I love your orange hair!"

Then turning and gesturing to our Honoured Visitors from Ghana, she excitedly declared,

"You must be so happy, Aunty Carrie; your Mum and Dad have come!"

THE END

5

The Lesson Lesson

"Welcome to your Lesson Lesson!"

That's how my Teacher first introduced us to her History Class. I have often wondered if it was more about *how* she taught rather than *what* she taught that caused my love affair with History; particularly my love of dates.

Did you enjoy History at school or were you like many of my classmates who groaned at the thought of Triple History for the last three periods on Friday afternoon? If you were, you weren't like me. I loved learning about Days of Old, Knights of Old and Kings and Queens of Old: anything and everything to do with the Past thoroughly engaged my thoughts, attention and imagination.

Thus, for me, Triple History was bliss.

My Tutor always brought history alive for me, it was an interchange between her and me: not just her droning on with boring facts and figures and me pretending to be listening, while my mind and heart were looking forward to my other passion, my next netball match. She spoke so enthusiastically and graphically that I used to feel I had actually witnessed and experienced the famous historical events she described.

You know: I was there when Sir Francis Drake was finishing off his game of Bowls on Plymouth Hoe before he defeated the Might of the Spanish Armada, on behalf of the British people, on 29th July, 1588.

I was there when King Harold II received the fatal arrow in his eye at the Battle of Hastings on 14th October, 1066.

I stood beside Anne Boleyn, to comfort her, as she mounted the scaffold before her execution on 19th May, 1536.

My Instructor had this clever knack of applying these historical events to modern day life. She would ask us how we felt things could have been thought out better, carried out better and would have worked out better, had they been done another way. She would constantly say there was no point in her teaching us things that happened long ago (or recently, even), if we weren't going to benefit in our own lives from them and learn from other people's past mistakes and fatal errors: not forgetting joyful, successful happenings as well, of course! She said History Lessons had to be truly that: **lessons** or warnings for us, that we might avoid making similar bad judgements and bad decisions and ruin our own lives. Hence she called them Lesson Lessons. No wonder I loved History. She made me think it was all about me!

Here I am now, married and a mother but still as fascinated as ever by History.

Five months ago, I was sitting next to my best friend in a plush, North Country Cinema, enthralling at a special showing of the World-Acclaimed Film, '**The King's Speech**'.

When the Performance was over, I stepped out of the warmth of The Odeon and into the cold night air. I shuddered but that was more from reflection than temperature. One particular element of the Film, the one that portrayed King George VI's debilitating speech impediment as being brought about by his father, George V's harsh treatment toward his children, was the part that troubled me.

With much to think about, I didn't want to go straight home so I asked my friend if she fancied a walk down to the Sea. I needn't have asked, really, as I am fully aware of her love of the beach: it almost matches mine!

Silently, we walked along to the end of Rigby Road and crossed over on to The Promenade.

"I wonder if this is where King George V stood," I remarked nonchalantly, stopping and stretching out my arms as if measuring the exact spot.

"What are you on about?" my companion queried.

31

"On the 8th July, 1913, the King visited Blackpool with his wife Queen Mary."

"Wow! Today is the 8th July, 2011!"

"I know," I sounded very serious, "exactly 98 years from today, The Ruler of The British Empire stood here!"

My lady-mate stood back respectfully as if the ground on which she stood was sacrosanct.

"It might not have been exactly right here," I cautioned, "but it was on The Prom, so it could have been."

"I'm confused, why would The King and Queen be here then? Why weren't they in London, encouraging all their people, their loyal subjects, who were embroiled in The Great War all over the Empire, to be strong? I think it's a poor show, the Monarch enjoying a day at the seaside with all the fun of the fair when all the world, his world, was at war!"

I looked at her very sombrely, trying desperately not to grin.

"Yes, it is a poor show that a living subject of that Empire doesn't even know the dates of that Great War."

"What do you mean?" she raised her perfect eyebrows.

"**You** obviously didn't listen well enough in History to know the dates of the First World War!"

"It started in 1912, didn't it?"

My friend leaned over the newly painted railing and looked out across the shore to the sea.

"You have been watching too much Sea!" I laughed. "1912 was the year The Titanic went down. World War 1 began for Great Britain on August 4th, 1914, the year **after** King George V's visit to Blackpool."

She turned and chuckled, "I knew that!"

"Seeing '**The King's Speech**'," I said very solemnly, "made me realise the heavy responsibility we parents, all parents, bear in raising our off-spring successfully. I have always tried to be a balanced mother: loving, caring, as well as guiding our young, directing them wisely by both word and example. Seeing how our last King turned out, made me so sad. I doubt King George V, his father, realized the terrible consequences of his harsh actions on his son. I just hope we have done it right! It is such a paradox that in history we read about severe kings producing indulgent fathers in their own children and the opposite: permissive kings producing Tyrants in their children!"

"So you think children become the opposite of their parents?" My friend frowned.

"They seem to: well, History seems to point to that when it comes to Royalty."

"No need to worry then," she laughed.

The dilemma in my mind was, as my husband and I were so differently brought up, together our own child-rearing skills made up a very mixed cocktail of strictness and leniency. He'd been a spoilt, cosseted child, practically bubble-wrapped by his doting parents: protected from everything possible and given anything possible; yet, when it came to his own brood, our children, as a father, he was harsh and unyielding. He seemed to say, "No!" to all of their requests: something I found very puzzling.

My father, quite the antithesis of my father-in-law, had been a totalitarian dictator (well, my brother and I thought so), denying us everything. He even marched us down to the Police Station when he caught us giggling about our escapade in scrumping apples from Reverend Pilkington's orchard! Perhaps suffering from such Draconian treatment encouraged my much more lenient, laid back attitude to parenting.

From our early days as parents, I was determined to counteract and compensate for my husband's strict handling of our twins, which resulted in me probably becoming overprotective and over indulgent, showing them boundless love and giving them almost unending attention. My intent was to mould two well-balanced and Great British

Citizens between us. I pondered long and hard, trying to draw on the lesson History might teach us in our case, knowing it is something we can learn from, something that can help us to avoid the pitfalls of the Past.

Which way would our children incline, I wondered?

It was not that our teenage twins were particularly troublesome, anyway. Our quiet daughter was a dream. We shopped together; me buying her everything she wanted that my part-time salary could stretch to (although she rarely asked for much). We spent many a 'Mum and Daughter' evening splodging our faces with thick, green Lush concoctions to produce perfectly soft skin; trying desperately not to laugh at each other resembling green-faced monkeys. We would watch soppy films together and laugh, sigh and cry and we would spend hours talking about school, boys and makeup in the bathroom at night, while cleansing our faces and cleaning our teeth.

Our son was more of a handful and I must admit, I was slightly more strict with him but he was a boy, after all. 'High-spirited' perfectly described his sunny and cheeky disposition. His choice of friends often disturbed me, however, and I often worried they might form a Gang but then, when I expressed any concerns, he would hug me and reassure me, that really wasn't his 'scene'.

Recently, he asked my husband if he could have a new hoodie: a fleecy track suit top, complete with a snug hood, which is seen hanging from or covering over the head of many a youth today. This was met with the usual refusal, so my son pleaded with me. His appeal wasn't necessary, as I could see neither rhyme nor reason as to why he couldn't be granted such a simple request, especially as he had been suffering from nagging toothache of late, which really put him out of sorts. The Dentist reassured us it was purely his wisdom teeth coming through but the pain became pretty severe at times. Consequently, I was found in town the next day, searching the stands of hoodies in the Sports Shop. Their exorbitant prices staggered me.

I began to reason that perhaps my husband was right to quash such an expensive application, when a bright poster, high in the sky of the shop caught my eye. '**Less than Half-price Sale**'! I raced to the rack at the back of the store and began rummaging for that unique bargain. I sifted through the stand, hanger by hanger until I spied exactly that, for which I searched.

Thrilled with my buy, I left the shop and hurried home to start on the necessary repair work as soon as I could. The assistant explained that it had been caught on a metal hook, ripping a hole in the pocket. I neatly sewed on a badge, not an ordinary badge but one belonging to my son's favourite football team, Manchester United, and covered over the tear in the pocket. An ingenious move, as when I gave it to him, my lovely boy was elated. I left the original price tag attached to the hoodie.

"You spoil that boy, rotten," was my husband's initial comment, "and what on earth possessed you to buy him something red? Isn't that a bit effeminate for him?"

"Don't be such a Grumpy Old Man!" I laughed, refusing to let his father spoil our son's moment. "Everyone in Britain knows Manchester United are known as, 'The Reds'!"

Undaunted, our son went off to show his new, prized possession to his friends.

Life, as well as History, is an unexpected Teacher, though; a profound and frank Professor, indeed, and I remember every detail with pain and sorrow of how, not long after this, I became its hapless pupil with regard to our children's upbringing.

My faithful friend and I were sitting in a bijou teashop just across the road from the famous Blackpool Beach. It was a charming café with small round tables covered in green, gingham table cloths, each one having pots of pretty fresh flowers on top. We had managed to bag the one table nestled right in the window, affording us a marvellous, uninterrupted, panoramic view of the shore we both so loved.

I lifted the lid of the white, porcelain teapot and plunged in a teaspoon to stir up the hot water. I breathed in deeply and sniffed the intoxicating aroma of the brew, which, accompanied by the comforting clinking of the rotating spoon on the china, was bliss!

"Hmmmm, English Breakfast: perfect," I whispered, noticing the two labels of the teabags, dangling on strings like thin tentacles down the rounded sides of the teapot, "my absolute favourite!"

My knowing friend laughed, "Anything English and you are away!"

"Not necessarily!" I frowned, as I poured the tea into the two large, beautiful, white, porcelain cups; they, to me, were simply perfect, too, plain but elegant.

Just as I was about to take my first taste, I glanced outside and saw a tall figure walking along the footpath towards the teashop. He wore a long, light beige, trench coat, neatly fastened at the waist by a wide, buckled belt and his head was covered in a stylish, brown Trilby. He appeared such a dichotomy as he held his body so straight and with such dignity but he had to be assisted in his unsteady gait by a walking stick; albeit an impressively carved one.

Suddenly, coming up from behind the tall man, came a group of unruly, noisy, hooded youths who didn't appear to see him and simply bludgeoned their way past him, one of them blatantly kicking his walking stick away from him and knocking him to the ground. The man's hat flew into the air and he ended up prostrate on the pavement. The callous offenders simply laughed and ran off, shouting,

"Stupid Old Granddad! Silly Old Man: look where you're going!"

Sickened, we immediately pushed back our chairs and ran outside to his aid, quickly followed by the Manager of the teashop. We asked him if he was hurt anywhere. He shook his head, so we carefully helped him back on to his shaky feet then, walking either side of him and supporting him under his arms and elbows, we gently guided him back into the shop and sat him in a chair up to our table. My companion went back outside and picked up his hat and walking stick, while the Manager made him a pot of freshly brewed tea and carried it over to our table on a tray with a gleaming clean cup and saucer. I didn't say a word. I just poured him out a cup of steaming tea; the cure-all for times such as these, methinks.

"Milk?"

"Just a dash, thank you," he replied in a beautifully articulated English accent.

"Sugar?"

"No, thank you."

I added the preferred measure of milk and placed the cup and saucer close to him. His hand trembled as he lifted up the spoon to stir in the milk. I wished I had done that for him. I tried not to but I worried he might not have the control to lift up the large, round cup, I so admired. He attempted to pick up the cup with one hand but then quickly reinforced his grip by using both of them, which shook so severely, I was scared he would spill the hot tea and scold himself.

"So," I said bravely; trying desperately to avert the attention from his evident, weak grasp, "what do you do, then?"

The man remained silent and took a sip of his tea, which was swirling about in his cup like a little storm at sea, agitated by his tremor.

"You must do something," I pressed on.

The man looked blankly across the table, hardly raising his head and said nothing. My friend shot me a staring glare, willing me to stay mute but I am hopeless at that. ((Come on, I am a Writer))!

"Tell us what you are," I coaxed.

The man finally looked up and for the first time, I could see his beautiful face. Even though the toll of time had taken its fee with the deep lines that cradled his mouth and eyes, he was still so incredibly handsome. I was so taken aback by his rugged, good looks that I broke out into a wide smile. The man smiled back and I relaxed.

"Persistent, aren't you?" he chuckled.

"More like, nosey," laughed my girl friend.

The man turned and smiled at her, too.

"So," I asked again, "what do you do? Who are you?"

"Who am I?" he smiled again. "I am Mr. Nobody."

"Yeah right, and I believe you, speaking in The Queen's English to perfection," I chuckled.

The man laughed back at me with a glint in his eye and I knew that even now, despite his advancing years, he still had the skill and the desire to charm a woman and with such ease!

"I am…..I was…..a Barrister," he stated.

"My, my," I commented, "you must have seen some great changes in your life, then: some great action?"

The man looked down again, which disappointed me and made me feel so responsible for, unwittingly, asking such an obviously painful question. I tried another tack.

"Forgive me for appearing rude but did you live during the War?"

The man didn't lift up his head. Once again, I glanced at my friend who shot me a warning look, which I totally ignored, of course.

"What did you do in the War?" I pushed.

The man continued in his silence.

"Would you like some more tea?" my vexed mate ventured.

The man shook his head.

I had such a strong feeling there was so much more to this man and as I was very, very inquisitive, I had to find out what! Even though the offer of more tea had been declined, I poured out another, added a dash of milk, stirred it in and then pushed the replenished cup towards him. To my surprise, the man lifted up the large cup, only this time with much more ease, far less shaking and he took a little sip.

"Thank you," he laughed.

"Are you going to tell us what you did in the War, then?" I smiled. "Were you a Spy or something?"

"No, not a Spy: a Pilot."

On hearing his words, everyone in that tiny teashop fell silent.

"A Pilot, what did you fly?"

"A Spitfire: I was a Spitfire Pilot."

The silence was broken only by everyone gasping.

"Wow," I shook my head, "did you go on many raids?"

"I am afraid I did; I was a Squadron Leader."

Again, all of the audience in that little café noisily drew in their breath. The man's voice, although quiet, was very commanding and carried over to all the eager and intensely respectful and attentive ears.

"Do you know what day it is today?" he asked.

"I do," I replied, as if I was back in my History Class again. "It is the 3rd September 2011, which is exactly 72 years since the outbreak of the Second World War in Europe."

The man smiled. "I'm so glad some people remember," he said quietly; remaining still and silent for at least a minute.

Nobody in that Tea House spoke; it was as if they were joining him in a minute's respectful silence.

Then he began..........

"I watched my Men blown to pieces in the skies. I watched them burn alive in their tiny cockpits. I saw them bale out over the Channel or France and I hoped upon hope that they would be safe. I visited the ones who made it back, either in the Mess or in the RAF Hospitals. I saw, once-handsome young men with half their faces burnt off. I saw my terrified but courageous Men without arms or legs. All of them, without exception, were young and eager and not one moaned about their injuries or losses. Most of them, if they could talk, would laugh through their bandages and say things like, "Pretty hard cheese, Sir.""

"I would still be writing to the families, desperate for news of their brave young men; fathers, husbands, brothers, cousins, uncles, sometimes at two and three o'clock in the morning. Those who received my letters knew the news would only be bad: either, 'Missing, presumed dead' or 'Killed in action'.

"You have no idea how hard those letters were to write. Nobody wanted this War but we gave of ourselves and despite the overwhelmingly heavy losses, we finally won and all of us would do it all over again if asked to: and why? So that those youths, those ones who just knocked me over, might be able to live in freedom: in a Britain that is free of Tyranny, Cruelty, Oppression and Suppression."

The Silence in that little tea shop was so loud it deafened us all.

I was so mad, so blooming mad, so livid that, despite the stinging tears rolling down my cheeks, I wanted to go and find those foolish youths. I wanted to sit them down, not in front of a screen, where they played 'pathetic fighting games' on their computers or mobile 'phones (no doubt every one of them was so good at those), but I wanted them to experience the real thing. I wanted to strap them, alone, in the tiny, cramped cockpit of a Spitfire and I wanted to hurl them into the angry, red, raging skies, shadowed by deadly, black war clouds. I wanted to blast off their ears with the horrific droning of a chasing Messerschmitt or the dreaded Stuka and I wanted them to hear the deafening sounds of machine gun fire, ricocheting all around them, rocking and shaking their little planes so that they clattered and rattled like giant tins of metal nuts and bolts. I wanted them to experience, to taste, just a tiny, tiny piece of the terror that this man and all of the men who served so valiantly, felt. I also wanted those obtuse, mindless hooligans to understand, to comprehend that these gallant, forgotten heroes did it all so selflessly, so uncomplainingly, just to give these senseless young people a future and such freedom!

I was so angry, seething with rage and I had every reason to be so!

Later, I walked home, completely confident that what I had done was exactly the right thing to do.

When I got in, my son was sitting in an armchair in the Front Room, cradling his face in his hands.

"Where have you been, Mum?" he asked, sounding as if he had something far too big in his mouth. "I've been sending you texts and ringing you all day but you haven't replied to or answered any of them; not one! You would really moan at us if we did that to you."

I took the mobile telephone out of my bag and saw all the unopened texts and 'missed calls' listed on the screen.

"My toothache was so bad this morning and my face was so swollen that Matron telephoned the Dentist. He told me to come in straight away but as I couldn't get hold of you, I 'phoned Dad and he left work then and there, picked me up from school and took me in. Great Mum you are!"

"What did you say?" I was horrified.

"It's all right, Mum, no need to panic, I still have my wisdom teeth but along with them, I have a nasty big abscess and it's still pretty painful. The Dentist gave me an anti-biotic jab that hurt like hell but he said it was much quicker than taking tablets. I'm no good at doing that, anyway: you know that!"

"But this can't be," I said with foreboding, "I saw you in town about an hour and a half ago," oh, was I panicking!

"No, you didn't, Mum, don't be so silly. I went to school, then the Dentist's, then home."

"No, no, I clearly saw you. I was sitting in a teashop when you and your mates went past, don't you remember knocking over an old man; YOU particularly?"

"Mum, what are you going on about? Ask Dad, I haven't been in town today: just to the Dentist in Cleveleys."

I kept shaking my head.

Ten minutes later I was in the kitchen, my mind agitated beyond imagination, making the needed cup of tea, English Breakfast, of course, when the key was heard in the front door lock.

"What's to eat, Mum?" my daughter's sweet voice was heard in the hall, which lightened my troubled mood as it always did.

"Fancy some cheese on toast?" I said half-looking over my shoulder and smiling at her as she walked in brightly: she never failed to make me smile.

"I'd love some, Mum," she replied stepping forward and giving me a wonderful hug from behind me, leaning her head on my back, "you know it's my all-time favourite!"

"With Marmite on top?" I asked, as she still hugged me, and knowing the reply I would get.

"Mum!" she laughed, pulling away from me and looking round to my face, giving me one of her lovely smiles I so loved.

I rubbed her face gently and smiled back as only a loving parent can then I turned around and watched my daughter walk away from me.

She was wearing her brother's new, red hoodie with the Manchester United badge carefully sewn on the pocket.

How swiftly can a smile turn to stone?

"Love," my husband called down from the front bedroom, upstairs, "there is a Police Squad Car parked outside our house and there are two tall policemen walking up the garden path."

I was there when Solicitor, James Downs finished off his game of golf before facing the might of the British Legal System, on our behalf, on 3rd December 2011.

I was there when my husband received the arrow in his eye after hearing The Judge pass sentence on our daughter, at The Juvenile Court on 5th December 2011.

I stood beside my silent daughter, to comfort her, as she climbed the steps of her Juvenile Detention Centre on 7th December 2011.

THE END

6

Saint-Palais-sur-Mer

(I wrote this on the back of a receipt , using the same meter, the day after I wrote 'Saint-Georges-de-Didonne' I was with my three little granddaughters & my son-in-law: my daughter joined us later.)

Beach bordered parasols,

Yellow glows.

Paige, Elle, Beth, little dolls,

Naked toes.

Lemonade and Sancerre,

Glass clinks.

Blue bottled Eau de Mer,

Baby drinks.

Stacked tables, pram and crab,

Torn pickings.

Dressed salad, seems drab,

Prefers chickens.

Beach Players cheer and leap,

Loud laughter.

Night Bathers paddle deep,

Swimming after.

Waves crashing on creamy beach,

Moon glistening.

French folk using no speech,

Still and listening.

Long face with saddened brow,

Daughter missing.

Happy smiles, nuzzling now,

Lovers kissing.

Long limbs making hand stands

In the air.

Children play on the sands,

Saint-Palais-sur-Mer.

7

My Glenys

(I wrote this when I was asked by Christy Tillery-French, in an interview for Dames of Dialogue, what was the inspiration behind Award-Winning **Joni-Pip**).

I was born into a Middle Class, totally Anglo-Saxon Family in Bedfordshire, England. When I was eight, my parents moved us into a beautiful Edwardian Villa with fifteen rooms and three acres of fabulous garden. Of course, this meant I had to change schools. I was given an 'intelligence test' and was duly put into a class with eleven-year-olds.

As I was three years younger than the rest of the class, this meant that the girl, whose desk was adjoined to mine, was decidedly more mature, more sophisticated and unquestionably, more chic, than the wild, untamed Carrie; whom I couldn't help but be! She was called, Glenys and she was absolutely everything I so desired to become. 'Glenys'? How worldly did that sound, why her very name evoked experience, class and style. How different were we? She was quiet and judicious, while I was noisy and rash. She was rounded, not plump, with soft, white skin and her hands were padded and pliable, not like mine, scrawny, tight and always tanned from constantly being outdoors. Her hair was platinum blonde, neatly bobbed with no fringe and a metal grip that securely kept every hint of hair off her perfect face.

It wasn't just her appearance that was perfection; the interior of her desk was the personification of orderliness and orthodoxy! When she lifted up the lid of this embodiment of every teacher's dream, what wonders met the eye! All of her exercise books were neatly stacked in a symmetric pile, having the largest on the bottom and the smallest on the top. Her text books stood in a similar tower, mirroring the precision of a ziggurat. Lying in a regimented line, from shortest to longest, were her exquisitely pointed, perfectly sharpened pencils. Her set square, slide rule and compasses were placed carefully in one corner, alongside an assortment of absurdly clean erasers: clean, yes I did say, *clean* erasers:

come now…..is that really possible?

My desk, on the other hand, was ever so slightly different! When my lid was raised, a range of errant papers flew into the air! Everything lay jumbled in a chaotic mess, forming a wonderful cocktail of text books, broken pencils, grubby erasers and torn and crumpled exercise books. How I longed for my desk to be like that of my dearest friend, Glenys!

Our differences strayed also into the manner in which our bodies were shaped and attired. Her stout figure was always immaculately dressed: nothing ever seemed out of place. Her uniform couldn't have looked better. Her grey school skirt always hung in exquisite, even pleats. Her cardigan never lacked and never displayed undone buttons and her socks always stayed up, all the way, right to her chubby knees. She also wore, which I was particularly in awe of, a shiny, brown, small, leather purse on a long strap that stretched diagonally across her body; it reminded me of the banner our Queen sometimes wore. It gave Glenys such an Imperial look.

Sadly for me, I was the total opposite of the Majestic Glenys. I was this skinny rake with loads of feral, strawberry-blond hair. It was (and still is), never tamed. My parents were both Professionals, so they employed a Nanny to take care of me and she took great pains on my appearance before sending me off to school. I was always neatly coiffured in two regimentally organised plaits, securely tied up with red ribbons and I was smartly clad in a white blouse with a red and grey striped, neatly knotted necktie and a carefully buttoned up, knitted, red, woollen cardigan. Nanny also checked my long, grey socks were pulled up straight and my grey school hat was very firmly on my head (not to mention the effort and time she had taken, the night before, to ensure my sensible school shoes were so highly polished that she could clearly see her reflection frowning back at her in the toes). However, despite all these stringent endeavours to present me as a well-turned-out, well-cared-for and well-groomed pupil; invariably, I would arrive in the school playground, totally dishevelled, scruffy and oh, so grubby!

The problem was a simple one; it was all down to my love of Nature! Getting to school afforded me this wonderful walk through fields, teeming with wild flowers. Granted there was a block paved path that wended its way through these meadows but why would I use that when

I could plunge myself into the long, green grasses, heaving with masses of pink, white and purple Columbine, brilliant yellow sunbursts of Coltsfoot, white spray heads of Giant Hogweed and the mauve and white towers of Bear's Breech?......I could go on and on! It was nothing other than Flowers Ville, Bloomsbury or Scent City for me!

Columbine

Coltsfoot

Each day, I would be so busy gathering up a few precious samples of these beautiful flowers (to take home and press in the current book I was reading), that I would forget the time and it would only be when I heard the school bell tolling from across the field that I would realise, yet again, I was late. I would hastily stuff the flowers in my School Satchel and head off tout de suite; catching my hat, hair, skirt, socks and blazer on the trailing brambles, in the process. How ever many times I was scolded for not being in the Playground at the bell, it made no difference to my daily sojourns across the fields; even in the rain.........mud and all! As a child, I never understood why the teachers used to cast an 'almost smile' at me when I walked into the classroom, squelching across the beautiful parquet flooring in mud-caked shoes and with long grass stalks sticking out of my hair and my school bag. I think my academic achievements dispersed any serious concerns the teaching staff might have had about my tardiness: most fortunately for me!

Break times and Lunchtimes were simply wonderful as I spent them totally in the company of the Glorious Glenys! We used to pretend to be horses (yes, the equine sort), whinnying and neighing as we

48

trotted around the Playground. I simply adored school and highly esteemed my wonderful companion. Neither of us ever missed a day, we just loved being there and just loved being together.

Giant Hogweed   Bear's Breech

One Friday, I couldn't understand it, Glenys wasn't in school. I was lost and lonely and simply walked around the playground on my own. It was the only day I could ever remember, not enjoying school.

On Monday morning, taking the path to school, I got enticed, as usual, by the beautiful flora that beckoned me from amid the tall grasses. Over I went into the meadow. I remember quite clearly picking a handful of pretty coloured Campion and stacking it very carefully into my satchel; most unusual for me as stuffing and cramming was more my normal practice. Then came the dreaded tolling of the School Bell, resounding around me and reminding me that, once more, I had forgotten the time and reminding me, once more, that I was very late. I grabbed my hat and sprinted off!

I ran as fast as I could, across the field and back on to the path that eventually formed an alleyway between a shop in the High Street and Mrs. Hubbard's walled orchard. I legged it the last few hundred yards up towards my school, only to discover that, to my horror, as I approached the school gates I could see standing in front of the green, painted railings, none other than my Head Teacher. What mortification! I stopped dead in my tracks. My first thought was to turn around and run straight for the alley that led back to the meadows and hide in the soaring grasses but I dismissed that idea, as I loved school. I quickly plonked my school hat, very wonkily on my head, did up my buttons, pulled up my socks and made sure none of the delightful columbine was sticking out of my satchel. I decided that the best course of action was to keep walking and completely ignore The Iron Battleship that stood between me and my Port of Call. Attempting this brave feat, steaming on with head held high, I took a sideways glance, only to be disarmed by the look on Miss Major's highly made up, taut face. She always struck terror in my heart. She was the embodiment of Spinsterhood and only accepted excellence from her students, particularly 'Her Girls' and, oh joy, once more, I was late! However, she didn't scold, she didn't remonstrate; she gently put her head on one side, extended a very thin arm and smiled at me, very, very strangely.

"Carrie," she said quietly, encasing my muddy mitt within her beautiful, elegant hand with long, slender fingers and highly polished, scarlet painted, pointed nails.

She led me, bemused and uneasy, straight through the front door of the school and into, could you believe, the School's Holy of Holies, The Sacred Staff Room? This was a room no pupil would ever dare enter, normally. It was the unknown place; the secret space where we would try and catch a glimpse of one or two members of staff, smoking a cigarette, something we thought was really daring and totally exciting (how things have changed)! I remember looking round anxiously as Miss Major sat me down, very gently, on a huge, black armchair. The arms, either side of me, seemed to tower right up to the ceiling and I could smell the strong aroma of leather all around me. I looked straight ahead and saw familiar members of staff looking at me in such a peculiar way. I wondered what on earth was going to happen to me and for once, I, Carrie King, was lost for words; utterly speechless and chronically terrified.

I remember my Headmistress then getting on her knees in front of me and speaking very softly and as she did so, she systematically undid all of my buttons and re-buttoned up my cardigan that I had obviously done up the wrong way.

"Carrie," she whispered, "do you remember Glenys wasn't in school on

Friday?"

I nodded, not daring to speak. Was I allowed to, in this place of such sanctity?

"Well, unfortunately, she was very poorly but you know Glenys, she never complained."

I nodded again.

"It wasn't until Saturday that her Mother realised that Glenys was so ill."

I began to feel slightly perturbed, which Miss Major obviously sensed and as, by this time, all of my cardigan buttons had been duly pulled through the correct holes, she took both of my hands in hers.

"By the time the doctor was called, Glenys was very ill, indeed," she continued then she took in a deep breath. I can still hear that air being dragged into her lungs, it was so loud. "She was rushed, in an ambulance, to Luton and Dunstable Hospital but sadly, Carrie, so sadly, she had a condition called Peritonitis. It was her appendix, you see, it needed to be taken out, as it was poisoning her body………but it was too late."

My heart within my little bony ribcage felt like lead, it was so heavy but still I said nothing, dreading what was to come next.

"I am so sad to have to tell you this, Carrie……" the melted Iron Maiden paused, bit into her top lip and took in another immense breath of air, "……but Glenys died yesterday."

I remember feeling nothing. The silly words this silly teacher was saying meant nothing, absolutely nothing. I remember jumping off that big chair and pulling my hapless mistress out of the Staff Room, across the corridor and into my classroom. The room was empty. I dragged Miss Major over to my desk, pulled out my chair and pushed her awkwardly down on it. I then sat down next to her on Glenys' chair and pulled it up to her desk.

"Don't worry," I said, "Glenys will be here after Assembly. It's all right, she is singing, 'All things bright and beautiful', with the rest of the school, can't you hear her? She's in the Hall, right now." I then raised Glenys' immaculate desk lid, "See, everything is waiting for her! You have got it all wrong, she is not dead! It is fine, she will be here!"

I remember the tears running down Miss Major's face as far as her ruby red lipstick. I stretched my hand forward and touched the tears.

"Don't cry, Miss Major, please don't cry. She will be coming in, in a minute, you'll see! We will have lessons, it's Monday morning, it's fine...we will work hard, as we always do and then we will have our bottle of milk and then we will go out into the playground......" I remember the tears. I didn't want them to come. I didn't want to feel anything and as they started to stream down my face, I kept brushing them away. ".......then we will play horses: we know it's silly but we don't care, we love it......" I continued, hardly able to speak coherently, "......she will be here in a minute......we just have to wait. I won't pick wild flowers anymore. I will come straight to school. I have some in my satchel but they are the last ones. I won't be late. I won't be late!" I shouted and I remember babbling on and on until, finally, the tide that I had been hoping to stem, could be held back no more and the floodgates burst open!

I sobbed and groaned and my compassionate Headmistress stood up and pulled me into her, cuddling me in a way that I didn't think was possible for her. I didn't recognise this new creature. She was no longer the strict, unyielding, authoritarian I had always known her to be: she became this gentle, soft Comforter, stroking my hair and gently rocking me from side to side.

Miss Major did not leave me for one single moment during all of that truly hideous and horrible day.

I learnt later that her secretary had telephoned my parents to come and pick me up but they were away on business and it was my Nanny's day off. Therefore, at four o'clock, I was honoured to be ushered into the passenger seat of Miss Major's delightful, little green Morris Minor and she drove me home.

I wasn't allowed to go to my best friend's Funeral. 'They' (whoever 'they' might be), thought it would not be 'good for me'. I was so upset but no amount of begging or pleading would change my parents' minds.

A Beautiful little Morris Minor

Glenys was buried in our village Church. As soon as school was finished on the day of her funeral, I went to the Churchyard and found the fresh mound of earth that displayed a primitive wooden cross with the words, 'Our Glenys', written on it. I clearly remember the smell of the newly tossed earth as I lay beside my best friend. I presumed they had placed the temporary cross at her head.

The mound was quite tall but I remember putting my arm over it as high as it would stretch. I spoke to my friend and I told her that I was so sad that I wasn't allowed to go to her funeral but that I would never, ever stop thinking about her ((and to this very day, I never have)).

I had already stopped picking flowers in the mornings but that day, the day of the funeral, I went to the fields after school and picked some pretty, yellow cowslips. I had put a tall, glass fish paste pot from the conservatory into my satchel before I left for school that day. There was an old tap in the Churchyard, so I filled up the pot with fresh water and placed the flowers for Glenys, by her head.

There were other flowers there, of course but I pushed them to one side so she could see mine. I didn't return home from school on time, that day, so my frantic Mother came searching for me. I remember her calling my name from across the other side of the wall. It took me a little while to register, as I was talking to Glenys and telling her what she had missed at school. I clearly remember lifting up my head and seeing my Mother's face, peering over the top of the grey, moss-mottled Churchyard wall. She wasn't cross, she told me she was just worried. We walked down the hill together, hand-in-hand; I could not stop talking about Glenys. Our house was in the same road as the Church, so I didn't feel that I had strayed off, at all.

My visits to the grave became a daily trip and I remember my Mother coming and hauling me away day after day. The favourite flowers that I picked for Glenys were violets. I would place these delicate little blooms in tiny, glass jam pots.

Cowslips   Violets

Although I never ever returned to picking wild flowers in the mornings on my way to school, I did pick flowers again but the only ones I ever picked were for Glenys.

Eventually, I was forbidden by my parents to go to the Churchyard, unaccompanied. I was devastated. I remember my Mother saying that 'four months is long enough and it has to stop'. She just didn't understand. Occasionally, on a Saturday, when it was my turn to go to the Bakers to buy some fresh, crusty bread for breakfast, I would steal into the graveyard and leave some flowers for Glenys. By then, she had a grey headstone. I didn't care for that, I much preferred the original mound, which smelt so beautifully of fresh soil.   ((Readers of **Joni-Pip** take note: remember Seamus' conservatory))?

As my parents were Professionals, they hired a woman to help in the kitchen. She used to cook the most delicious cakes. Once she had put the cake mix into the oven, she used to pick up a round kitchen 'timer' and twist the knob until it pointed to a 'twenty' symbol. Immediately it would tick like a clock and the knob would slowly move back up, anti-clockwise, until it reached the zero symbol and then it would ring like an alarm clock. This was the signal for Cook to take the cakes out and they would be baked to perfection (as well as smelling so yummy)!

Glenys' grave, which stands next to the tree, beside the Church.

Also, the grey, moss-mottled wall, over which my mother looked and called me to come home.

The first time I watched our Cook do this, I asked her what she was doing and she said,

"I am 'setting the time' for 20 minutes."

I asked her why she had to twist the knob round the dial and she replied, "I am putting the 'time back'."

As the timer was circular, I asked her if Time was like a circle.

"Indeed it is!" she replied, "It just goes round and round all the time and we never have enough of it."

"Is that why you always say that you are running 'round and round in circles' and never getting anything done?" I asked.

"Absolutely!" she said very seriously.

A Circular Kitchen Timer ➜

From then on, every time she used the timer, I would say,

"Are you putting Time back? Are you putting the Circle back?" and Cook would answer, "Yes".

That got me thinking,

'What if I could, somehow, 'put the Time back, put the Circle back'? Then I could put it back to the Friday that Glenys was taken ill. I could take her to the Doctors on that very day and the doctor would send her to the Hospital and Glenys could have that nasty appendix taken out and she would be all better and not die!'

This thought constantly plagued me and a few years later, I went to the Library and looked up books about Time being 'put back'. The one I found that had the greatest impact on me was, 'The Time Machine', by H.G. Wells. That book astounded me, even though I was still so young. I determined, after reading it, that one day, I would fathom out how to put time back, put the Circle back and get Glenys back.

Well, I didn't discover the secret of The Circle of Time and how to put Time back, of course but the memory of My Glenys and my desire to save her from dying, continued so strongly in my heart and mind that I had to write about it, which I did, many years later in **Joni-Pip** (which, much to my surprise and delight, won a Book Award in The United States of America)!

THE END

NOTE: **The Life in the Wood with Joni-Pip** (ISBN: 9780955524691 or 9780955524615), is the first book in The **Circles** Trilogy and in it, although it is not Glenys (she, I have kept safely locked up in my heart), somebody does die and I have invented a way to 'put time back', so that they don't die. I have changed bad things in the Past by intercepting the Circle of Life and starting a New Circle and I have turned them into good things for the Present and Future (with strange consequences, naturally)!

I think, also, if you read **Joni-Pip** and you have read this, too, of course, you will recognise other things from the story of 'My Glenys'.

I am so happy that **Christy Tillery-French**, of **Dames of Dialogue**, has given me the opportunity to finally write down such poignant memories of my special friend, which gave me the inspiration behind the writing of **The Circles Trilogy**.

Thank you enormously, **Christy** and **Dames of Dialogue**! C.K.

8

Paris

(I wrote this in a café opposite the Arc de Triomphe).

Arc de Triomphe

Pretty parasols,

Wet pavements,

Bustle, bustle.

Stocked shops,

Designer labels,

Rustle, rustle.

People passing,

White tables,

Drinking, drinking.

Arty Artists,

Empty canvas,

Thinking, thinking.

Peaceful parks,

Chess games,

Playing, playing.

Tall trees,

Lovers kissing,

Laying, laying.

Busy boules,

Stretched arms,

Rolling, rolling.

Sandy circle.

Watching, waiting,

Bowling, bowling.

Fragrant flowers,

Long benches,

Talking, talking.

Children chatting,

Puppies pulling,

Walking, walking.

Manic Metro,

Crammed platforms,

Clinging, clinging.

Bold buskers,

Clear voices,

Singing, singing.

Sight seeing,

Camera flashes,

Grinning, grinning.

Roads raging,

Scary crossings,

Winning, winning.

Beaux bridges,

Wide river,

Flowing, flowing.

Satin Seine,

Open boats,

Going, going.

Faulty French,

Stumbled phrases,

Trying, trying.

Cappuccino coffee,

Crusty croissants,

Buying, buying.

Bright boats,

Tuilleries ,

Sailing, sailing.

Creaking chairs,

Hungry babies,

Wailing, wailing.

Paris places,

Eiffel Tower,

Touring, touring.

Looming La Defense,

Grand Arch,

Soaring, soaring.

Montmartre,

Sacré-Cœur,

Thirsting, thirsting.

Street sellers,

Crowded markets,

Bursting, bursting.

Darling daughter,

Feeling happy,

Wining, wining.

Tasty tasting,

French food,

Dining, dining.

9

Freedom

The old venetian blind swayed like a wave, to and fro in the welcome Summer breeze and knocked gently on the white painted window frame, while the carved, wooden knot holders on the end of the pull cords, tinkled like bells. Occasionally, a slat would part, casting shafts of sunlight across the classroom, stirring my fellow pupils from their illicit afternoon snooze: but not me.

Despite the unrelenting heat of that intensely humid day, I was enthralled by my Teacher's History lesson; a lesson that proved to be a turning point in my eleven-year-old life.

"**William Wilberforce** was so influential in the abolition of the slave trade in the British Empire," Miss Watson, my History Teacher, went on.

Learning about this man's passionate struggle to bring about great changes in the inhuman practice of buying and selling slaves, had such a massive impact on my heart, that from that day forth, I felt I carried on my little shoulders, the guilt of every white man walking. So strong was my disgust over this evil treatment of Africans that I would apologise to every black person I came in contact with. I was so ashamed of being white.

So vividly did the images of that balmy sunny day in school stay with me in my mind that nearly four decades on, it still seems but as yesterday.

Fifteen years later, still full of remorse over the Slave Trade, I was newly married and in Ghana, West Africa, when a friend asked if we would like to visit a Slave Fort. At first I declined but my husband said we must go. I was so apprehensive when we arrived that my husband suggested before we entered the Fort, we should take a stroll along the vast, deserted beach, where huge waves crashed relentlessly on the shore. It seemed such a paradox that a place of such beauty could also be a place of such misery.

After asking if I was now ready and receiving a nod (although, in all honesty, could anyone ever be ready for such a task), we took the steps along the concrete quay where we were told the Slave Ships docked to load up their human cargo. Our Guide then led us up to the faded, dirty white fort. I kept telling him I was so ashamed.

We were shown a dank room with a massive door and were told that up to 500 slaves were herded into this room overnight and they all had to struggle for air with only one small hole in the ceiling. In the morning it was rare that more than 200 had survived the night.

Something smacked as very wrong here, something very 'not British', I am not talking about humanity, in this instance: it simply did not make economic sense. If the British, as I was lead to believe, were the foremost Traders in human flesh, then why did they not care for their precious cargo?

We were then shown around the Fort and saw exhibits of chains and irons that shackled the desolate slaves together. I was in tears. I kept apologising to our Guide, who kept his cool in his white shorts and open-necked, short sleeved, cotton shirt.

He continued on with the tour, which finally took us into a huge hall with a highly polished, wooden floor.

"Were the Forts built specifically for the Slave Trade?" I asked.

"Not really, Ma'am," he replied matter-of-factly, "they were originally built as Markets; Trading Posts, where Africans brought along gold, mahogany and other local items, in exchange for clothing, blankets, spices, sugar, silk and many other things."

I stood in the middle of that massive hall, flanked by very tall windows, which reminded me of my old Victorian School and then I thought of that Venetian blind, blowing on my own tall, Schoolroom window and I remembered the remorse I had harboured in my heart for all those years. Already though, my mind was in turmoil as his answer to my question was not in keeping with how I had been taught History.

The enormous, empty room could have been a dance floor for all intents and purposes, having a stage down one end. There was also a construction which resembled the pulpit in our local church. I rudely pointed to it (my mother had always insisted, 'it is rude to point', anyway), and asked what that was for.

"That is where the Auctioneer stood, Ma'am," explained our Fort Host, "the slaves would be brought and displayed on the platform and Traders would bid for them."

"I suppose the one with the highest bid would buy them, then?" I inquired.

"Exactly so," the man replied.

I slowly spun myself around on the heels of my strappy sandals. The thought of dancing, wafted me away for a few moments, away from the horrors of this evil place, although in all truthfulness, nothing was fitting into my imaginations of this terrible trade, this terrible trade of which I was constantly expressing penitence.

In the course of this slow revolution, I saw a massive Mural on the far end of the hall, behind the stage, like a backdrop for a Play. I stopped twisting round and just stared at it.

My new husband asked me if I was feeling all right. I didn't reply. Then the images on the Mural fell as heavy blows on my already injured heart. The painting was very big and stretched from one end of the stage to the other, the figures almost being life size.

I marched across the hall, my heels clacking on the wooden floor and just stared at the picture, scrutinizing every detail. On the far left, mud huts with straw roofs were painted, with a few older villagers and tiny children and babies holding up their arms and wailing in grief, some men were on their knees imploring and begging for mercy. I wished I could jump into the painting, to comfort them and set the poor, bound people free.

The middle part of the illustration depicted the long line of captives: some with wooden posts bolted round their necks, which were attached to the following slave. Other poor creatures had metal rings around their necks, which were chained to the next in line. They all, men, women and children had irons clapped round their ankles and wrists and they had heavy chains joining them all together. Slave drivers, wielding whips and carrying rifles, forced these desolate people on to their horrific future. The weirdest part of the artist's work was how he had portrayed the surrounding countryside, with lush, green trees and pretty bushes; it stood in such stark contrast to this extreme misery. What a dichotomy!

On the far, right end of the picture stood a Slave Fort on a hill and then alongside the Quay was a sailing ship. A White man stood on the edge of the shore, wearing well-tailored clothes and a tall hat and in his hands he held a large wallet from which he was handing over a big stash of cash, to pay for his 'wares'.

After surveying this incredibly informative mural, I marched back down the wooden floor, my impractical heels clacking away again, grabbed the arm of our hapless Tour Guide and dragged him all the way back to where I had been standing in front of this giant picture. I did not let go of his arm.

"What the Hell do you call this?" I screeched, gesticulating rather rudely at a detail on the painting.

The man looked blankly at me. I heard my husband snigger all the way down from the other end of the hall; he just wasn't used to hearing my rage, or my language come to that. I ignored him.

Still clutching the arm of our unfortunate escort, I hauled him up the four wooden steps on to the platform and stationed him almost within kissing distance of the canvas.

"Explain!" I thundered, my voice echoing around the empty hall.

The Guide's eyes looked cautiously between my face and the colourful work of art that confronted us.

"I am not sure I understand that which you are asking Ma'am," he said gently.

"Er.......right," I started, slightly unnerved by his quiet response, "there are plenty of black Africans in this picture, plenty of them and I only see one white man at the end of the chain, the one paying, am I right or am I mistaken?"

"No, Ma'am, you most certainly are not."

"Right or mistaken?" I pushed my face very close to his.

"You are right there is only one white man in the painting."

I still held him very close.

"So where are the rest of the evil white men, then: the ones who landed on these shores and went around capturing and kidnapping all these pitiful people, then?"

I let go of his arm, which I am sure by now, must have painfully ached from my unrelenting iron-like grip, and I pointed to the line of slaves.

"And why are these men, wielding whips and carrying rifles, ALL black? I was always lead to believe, I was always taught that the white, nasty men sailed with soldiers from Britain to Africa and just pillaged the villages of humans, taking all whom they pleased and dragged them across the land to these forts and threw them into damp dungeons awaiting a fate worse than death, a living hell, in slavery!"

There was an uncomfortable pause.

"Am I wrong? Or has my heart and mind been loaded down by wicked lies?"

The Tour Guide turned and looked at me, quite tenderly, which took me aback a bit, yet again, I must confess.

"Ma'am I am a student at the University of Ghana and I am reading African Studies, this is just my part-time job. We Africans do not desire to hide the truth of our blame in this terrible trade in human flesh. This painting you see before you is an accurate depiction of what took place on African soil, it is exactly so. We, Ghanaians especially, do not wish to erm….whitewash History. "

My husband walked up to join us. Sensing my rapid breathing, he put his arm around my waist to comfort me.

"Africans have been enslaving one another since antiquity and selling their enemies to Arabs from long ago," the student went on. "The Europeans: The Swedes, The French, The Dutch, The Portuguese and The British, as well as The Brazilians, came to Africa much later. The Europeans came here originally for the gold, not the people! The thought of White Slave Traders carrying out raids is not feasible; they were highly prone to our diseases: Malaria, Yellow Fever and Typhoid. Why do you think Africa was called, 'White man's Grave'?"

"I can't believe what I am hearing and seeing," I shrieked, shaking my head.

The man gestured around the mural as if he was giving a guided tour of the scene.

"The Africans would be captured by Africans, then they would be marched across the country in a 'coffle' (a slave convoy), run by other Africans then sold by an African trader operating on behalf of an African Chief to be held in a 'barracoon' (a slave prison), run entirely by Africans, until a ship arrived. The men on that ship would be the first white faces involved in the process. Up to that point, it was usually an all-African operation. We have some personal accounts still, where the slaves say they were with Africans for half a year before they ever saw a white face. In fact, by the time the slave trade was abolished in the West, there were many more slaves in Africa (black slaves of black owners), than in the Americas."

"Why have all these lies been told? Why can't everyone hold up their hands and admit their part in this man-made tragedy? I am so mad! I am so blooming mad!" I shouted ((I think I used a stronger word))!

My husband tried to calm me down by urging me to listen to that, which this honest and articulate man had to say but I couldn't, I started to cry. My husband went to cuddle me but I pushed him away.

"You don't understand," I sobbed very loudly, "since I was eleven-years-old, I have felt the weight of the guilt of my race on my shoulders. It has robbed me of a proper perspective of these heinous crimes against human beings. I have been lied to and I have believed the lies without question. I have been deceived. I am crying for my childhood, imprisoned in these lies, this deceit. I am not condoning **anyone**, any European, any British Trader, any South American or North American who cruelly and inhumanely treated these pitiful people but I am **condemning** all those, every last one of them, who are not interested in hearing and telling the Truth of it all and deviously hiding it and I deplore all those not accepting their Race's part of the blame! Such cowardice, what are they afraid of?"

The Tour Guide responded quietly and so respectfully, despite my outburst.

"Ma'am, one day the truth will be told; you see, many Africans are ashamed, too ashamed to admit their country's guilt in this tragedy, this scar on the face of Africa. They especially find it difficult to own up even though they know it was an African idea and Africans began The Slave Trade in the first place!"

From then on, my life changed and I no longer apologised to every black person I came in contact with. I am so thankful I actually saw the truth for myself, which nobody can deny, in that painting in that Slave Fort in Ghana and I heard the truth with my own ears from that brave young Ghanaian, our Tour Guide.

Recently, Ghanaian Diplomat, Kofi Awoonor, wrote:

"I believe there is a great psychic shadow over Africa and it has much to do with our guilt and denial of our role in the Slave Trade. We, too, are blameworthy in what was essentially, one of the most heinous crimes in human history."

Freedom, for me, came in the most unexpected of places.

By the way, I asked our Tour Guide his name and he replied,

"Angel."

THE END

An African Slave Fort

An African Painting with not
a white man in sight

10

Anne's Farewell

I have a pleasant view, looking out over the Thames from my window. My heart is full, remembering wondrous times I have enjoyed travelling on boats up and down these sweet-bitter waters.

I hear children laughing and squealing with delight. I hope our beautiful Bess is playing, too. Now my husband has sole custody, it pains me so. I trust he will take good care of her and always see that raisins and currants are put into her rice pudding. The Council was quite clear: I am classed as an unfit mother and can no longer feature in her life. The Court granted my husband a swift divorce. I pray my daughter will understand how much I truly loved her and her father.

I have entreated the Chaplain to watch over her for me, she is so little but I have faith that she won't forget all that I have taught her.

My wonderful brother has gone now, my father has disowned me, my friends have abandoned me, I am totally alone. Constable Kingston has treated me kindly, even though he believes I am guilty.

I grieve for my dead son, whose sad demise begat all this wretchedness.

The doors open, a quiet crowd waits to watch. The guards now escort me; I smell apple blossom, it's hard to die on such a day so lovely but the time has come to take my leave of this world.

God save the King and our daughter, Elizabeth.

She will be Queen.

THE END

(If you do not know who and what this is about, then shame on you)! C.K.

11

Seen from the Beach (such a pun)

(I wrote this while I was sitting on the busy beach in Lyme Regis, Dorset. I was looking out across the shore to the famous curved Cobb and when I looked around me, the smells, the sounds and the sights all encaptured me. I simply love Dorset! I entered this poem into a competition and the Judge said she was sad there wasn't one rhyming poem in all the entries! Very interesting. CK)

The Cobb and Golden Cap
(by kind permission of www.visit-dorset.com)

Cobbled Cobb curling,

Slack sails unfurling.

Greedy gulls soaring,

Spent sailors mooring.

Packed pebbles crunching,

Cheeky child munching.

Crammed cafés booking,

Clammy chefs cooking.

Pale people laying,

Soggy dogs playing.

White wavelets lapping,

Bronzed babies napping.

Milling mums chatting,

Dads deftly batting.

Sun seekers glowing,

Body boards bowing.

Freckled friends eating,

Lost lovers meeting.

Close couples walking,

Giggling girls talking.

Barrack boys lobbing,

Bouncing Buoys bobbing,

Brass bandsmen playing,

Brown bodies swaying.

Men mackerel fishing,

Sad sweethearts wishing.

Sea swimmers splashing,

Wayward waves crashing.

Older men reading,

Younger men pleading.

Tasty tea sipping,

Tiny toes dipping.

Cornish cream licking,

Postcard pack picking.

Strappy shoes trying,

Souvenirs buying.

Ammonites finding,

Trilobites minding.

Salty sea gleaming,

Warm writer dreaming.......

Lyme Regis.

A Lone Gull over Lyme Regis' Harbour
by © Rebekah French

Lyme Regis

(My daughter and grandson in Lyme Regis eating Fish and Chips served in paper; a truly delicious, British Tradition!   May 2015: by kind permission of Kevin Goodluck).

Ammonite fossils found on Lyme Regis' Beach
(by kind permission of www.visit-dorset.com)

((I find Lyme Regis beach the most amazing beach I have ever visited))

12

A Turning Point?

When my gorgeous husband was killed, I fell immediately into a pit of such unfathomable depths that I saw nothing but black and felt nothing but pain. Fortunately or unfortunately, whichever way you look at it, I was a late baby, so I was mothered by my three older sisters (my oldest sister left home long before I ever had the chance to get to know her but still she sent me a monthly allowance: spoilt or what), and my youngest brother and I had all the privileges of life heaped upon us.

I then met and married my husband, who also treated me like a princess: so the spoiling continued. While my life was deliriously happy, it meant I never knew what it was like to fend for myself, which was not a good thing. I was crazy in love with a man who did everything for me (before he was killed I had never even put out a dustbin bag for the Refuse Collectors). I cooked and cleaned, obviously but I really didn't do anything else practically, such as my car maintenance; checking the tyres, topping up water and oil etc., not to mention cleaning it! He also said vacuuming was a man's job!

Consequently, when my lovely man just suddenly disappeared from my life, I floundered (the only positive thing I can possibly think about losing him, is that I finally became my own person and had to fend for myself), I hardly knew how to breathe without him! I'd sit all day in my dressing gown and watch hours of mindless television. I'd go to bed at two in the morning, get up at four, put on my dressing gown, switch on the television and stare at it. My poor daughters felt they had lost both of their parents.

One day, about eighteen months after my husband's death, I was watching some more mind-numbing television. It was a British Film, starring the amazing Sean Bean, messing up his life as a budding football professional.

During the story, this beautiful song came on and the words pierced my heart like an arrow and made me sit up with a start. I felt the singer was in my lounge and speaking to me personally and telling me to stop, stopping everything from moving on!

He sang:- *'I want to know, how does it feel, behind those eyes of blue? You've made your mistakes and now your heart aches, behind those eyes of blue. People may say you've had your chance and let it slip away, but hard as they try, there's a dream that won't die, behind those eyes of blue. Maybe once in a while there's a trace of a smile, behind those eyes of blue but it's painfully clear, there's a river of tears, behind those eyes of blue. You know life is too short for compromising. Take a hold of your dream and realise it. You know there's nothing left to stand in your way EXCEPT YOURSELF and I know, though your heart's full of pain that a hope still remains behind those eyes of blue.* (Paul Carrack — Eyes Of Blue).

I quickly checked the name of the artist and the name of the song as the Credits rolled up. I went upstairs, showered, put on some make-up and drove to Milton Keynes and walked into HMV. I asked if they had the track and was told it came from **Paul Carrack's Album, Blue Views**. I asked the assistant to play it, so he put the headphones on me and as I listened, I sobbed and cried. People around apparently saw me and asked the assistant what I was listening to. He played it again, only this time through the massive shop's sound system. (They sold lots of Paul's albums that day)! From those words, I realised that I was the only one standing in my way, so from that day, I got up and got on with getting on.

Two weeks later, I couldn't believe it; my friend, Keith, who worked at The Stables Theatre in Milton Keynes, said that Paul Carrack was performing for three nights! Keith arranged for me to meet Paul. What a thrill that was and how kind Paul Carrack was! I gave him a letter I had written to him, telling of the impact his words had on my sad heart. He wrote back the most beautiful letter, saying that hearing such things made all his work so worthwhile. We have since met a few more times and he still continues to encourage me. In the front of **Joni-Pip**, I have quoted some of Paul's words, only I have substituted 'eyes of green', as my eyes are green (I asked Paul first). It was a true Turning Point, indeed!

13

The Hay-Haired Boy & The Three Bears

(This was entered into a competition for a modern, London, Fairy Tale)

Once upon a street in Wood Green, London, stood a cottage belonging to three Bears: Fred Bear, Heather Bear (known as 'Ev Bear), and their baby, Edward Bear, sometimes called Ted Bear but usually called Teddy Bear.

One shining Sunday morning, as a special treat, 'Ev Bear made some porridge in the microwave. She put it on for too long so the hot pots of porridge were too hot to eat. Fred Bear said,

"While the porridge, Mummy Bear made, is cooling down, let's go for a walk to the Paper Shop and get a newspaper and pop: the paper for me, Daddy Bear, the colour supplement for Mummy Bear and the pop for Baby Bear."

So they set off. 'Ev Bear was supposed to lock the door behind her but she had left her key upstairs beside her bed on a hook near her book she was reading and she really couldn't be bothered to go and get it, so she left the door on the latch, pulled it up then walked on to catch up Fred Bear and Ted Bear on their way to the corner store at the edge of Forest Road.

A paper boy with a shock of hair like the Mayor, the colour of a haystack and very much resembling one, was cycling past the three Bears' pad when he saw the door was ajar. He got off his bike and knocked: nobody was there so he walked in, pushing his bike beside him. He released the latch and closed the door, parking his bike on the black and white floor.

He looked up and down and then around and walked into the kitchen.

On the table lay three bowls of porridge.

"Don't mind if I do!" he said, trying Fred Bear's bowl. "Blimey," he said spitting the porridge out, "this pot's too 'ot! Manky muck!"

He then tried a spoonful of 'Ev Bear's porridge, which he also spat out.

"Would you believe it?" he asked, "This pot aint 'ot, it's bloomin' cold! Nasty!"

He then tried Teddy Bear's porridge, which was in a purple, plastic baby bowl, using a matching purple, plastic baby spoon. He said gleefully, in-between mouthfuls,

"Just the ticket!" and ate the lot.

He then sat on Fred Bear's best chair but it was too hard so he tried 'Ev Bear's armchair but it was too soft. Sitting on Teddy Bear's baby chair felt just right. Sadly, though, despite the Hay-haired boy being a little bloke, his weight was too much for baby Bear's chair so the spindly straight legs cracked and they broke.

The strawberry-blonde boy with the haystack-like head of hair then clonked up the bare stairs in his big boots because boys' boots are big, although this boy's boots were a bit too big and went bump, bump, bump as Fred Bear had never got round to putting the stair carpet down. He wanted to have a butcher's at the Three Bears' bedrooms.

In the first of the three Bears' rooms he pulled back the duvet and got into Fred Bear's roomy big bed: that was too hard.

He wandered into the second of The Three Bears' bedrooms and as he passed 'Ev Bear's dressing table he caught sight of his reflection in the mirror, not something he saw very often. It was a bit of a shock to see the shock of hair he had on his head, a bit of a shock, indeed.

"Flippin' ding dongs," he said out loud, "no wonder me ol' man says to me ol' woman, 'That lad's the spittin' image of Boris Johnson*. You been up to no good?' Silly ol' man, as if me Mum would!"

The Hay-Haired boy then got into 'Ev Bear's bed but that was too soft.

Finally, in the third of the three Bears' bedrooms he climbed into Teddy Bear's baby bed and that was as comfy as they come.

"Snug as a bug I bloomin' am!" said the golden-haired boy to himself and promptly fell into a deep sleep as he had been delivering papers since five that morning and was now plum-tucker-tired.

Soon the Three Bears arrived back from the paper shop but Fred Bear never said, "Who's been eating my porridge?"

or

"Who's been sitting on my chair?"

or

"Who's been laying in my bed?" even.

And why not? Simple.

Because they couldn't get back into the bloomin' house.

The moral of this story is:

'Don't leave your door unlocked in case Goldie locks you out!'

THE END

* Boris Johnson is the current Mayor of London (2015), renowned for his shock of unruly, golden-blonde hair.

14

The Matter of Spring

Isn't it easy to unshakably cleave to one's principles when things are going well but isn't it another matter, entirely, when things are not?

This was forcibly illustrated in 'The Spring Affair', when my beloved father's steadfastness was sorely tested. Born in 1924, he was only twelve when, much to his dismay, the King of England forsook his throne and country, abdicating for the woman he loved. This had such a lasting impact on his life, generating a staunch adherent to Peter Druker's words, **'Never mind your happiness; do your duty'.**

The Matter of Spring?

It all began, when, as a Senior Geological Engineer, my father was contracted to resolve some maintenance difficulties with the famous, or is it infamous, Akosombo Dam in West Africa (judging by all the problems this construction has brought upon the hapless people of Ghana, I have to wonder).

I was enjoying a Gap Year before going on to Oxford. Having spent the previous two years, cramming, revising, losing sleep and having no social life on account of my A Levels, I decided I needed a rest, a diversion from anything remotely study-related. I chose to do voluntary work in fulfilling pursuits at home, thus, lazing by the pool, playing tennis, shopping in Knightsbridge and sleeping, became the order of the day, for fifteen days, anyway.

My father then proposed it would be a great experience for me (character-building was the word he also used), to join him during his remaining three months in Ghana. Initially, I baulked at the invitation; this was not recovery; this was industry! I knew my father well; he was Alexander Garador, the eminent, Anglo-American Scientist, brought up and educated in Bath, England and earning a Master's Degree in Geological Engineering at Oxford. 'Brain Box', hardly skimmed the skin of his description.

Thus, ten days later found me doing my 'duty' at Heathrow Airport, looking back forlornly at my frantically waving mother and two brothers, until I turned a corner into Passport Control and lost their comforting sight. I felt alone for the very first time in my life.

After a turbulent flight, I was met by a driver at Accra Airport and soon was travelling North East towards my destination. The way the heat hit me when I first stepped out of the aircraft and breathed in Ghanaian air, reminded me of the time I first cooked a roast dinner. I'd opened the oven door to check my culinary masterpiece and put my head, all but, in the cooker. Now, however, I was travelling in the back of an extremely comfortable, air-conditioned Mercedes. Such relief from that heat!

Beginning the two-and-a-half-hour journey, afforded me glimpses of this unknown country. Very few vehicles were on the uneven roads (fortunately, though, keeping my tired bones unshaken, posed no problem for a Mercedes with superb suspension), but cyclists a-plenty braved the rough and bumpy ride on rusty, sit-up-and-beg bikes: some seemingly held together with hardly more than paper clips. The roads were bordered by stalls with street traders selling their wares from live chickens to ready-peeled oranges (such an extreme luxury for me: one who finds peeling an orange such a tiresome pursuit for such a deliciously fruity fruit)!

Along the way on both sides of the road, there were a few larger buildings and detached houses, surrounded by tall fences but the majority of dwellings were one storeyed, mud-brick houses.

I fought to stay awake but the flight had proven exhausting, so, in no time, the car ground to a standstill; I opened my eyes and we were there. The driver left the car, leaving the engine running and disappeared into a large, glossy, glass building, which seemed not in keeping with my images of Ghana.

Soon I spied my adored father walking towards me in his cream shorts and light blue, open-necked, short-sleeved shirt. In his early forties, he was so handsome and still had the look of a much younger man: I was so proud of him. I just couldn't wait for him to reach the car door so I leapt out into the oven and launched myself into the comfort of his outstretched, loving arms.

"Libby, you are here! How wonderful! How was the flight: much turbulence? Did you see any of The Sahara? Come in, we have food. Did you eat on the plane? What was British Airways' tuck like: muck like or good?"

I laughed. *However homesick I might get*, I thought, *I know being around him will make me happy.*

Within minutes we were sitting in an elegant apartment, whose wide windows provided us with wonderful views looking out over Lake Volta. One of the advantages of having a clever father was that he always managed to get excellent accommodation for the duration of his work.

After supper, I was shown into my beautiful bedroom. Alas there were no Mosquito nets hanging over the bed and I couldn't hear the roar of wild animals or the chirping of crickets! What a bitter disappointment! The driver carried in my luggage and I unpacked straight away. As Ghana is in the same Time Zone as the United Kingdom, I felt it was acceptable to have a shower and fall into bed at nine o'clock. My mother had awoken me at four that morning, so I was 'plum-tucker tired', as my much-missed Great Grandfather Garador used to say in his smooth American accent.

On our first morning, my father drove us to Akosombo and spent all day showing me around the Dam, he explaining how amazingly it worked. I understood very little but the views across the Lake were spectacular. English Literature was my subject: a scientist I was not!

We enjoyed the evening, talking and laughing about the times we spent at Knotty Knook, his parents' country cottage in Nottingham-shire: being in his company, always made me feel so safe and secure. I also loved the fact that my joining him made him so happy as nothing pleased me more than doing things that pleased him.

The following day, whilst still at breakfast, a loud knock came on the apartment door and in walked a tall, broad-shouldered, incredibly handsome man.

"Libby, come and meet your Tour Guide."

The man came over, extending his hand to shake mine.

"This is Spring," my father announced.

Our view of Lake Volta and The Akosombo Dam

"Spring?" I repeated in the highest pitch I think my vocal cords could possibly reach. This painful squeal was closely followed by a snort that even a charging warthog would be proud of. I inadvertently ignored his outstretched hand as, for obvious reasons, his dichotomous name entertained me immensely. Daddy shot me a disapproving but pointless look. Attempting to smother my mirth brought about an avalanche of groans and grunts that forced an escape into the bathroom. It probably wasn't particularly funny; nevertheless, the more I thought about this butch-looking man's branding, the more I dissolved into deep pits of aching laughter. I felt in danger of rupturing either several blood vessels or my sides.

Before long, I was sitting comfortably in the back of the Mercedes. The hilarity had been calmed and the control had been collected. I daren't look at the driver and most definitely daren't think about his name. I paid no attention, at all, to my surroundings but spent the whole journey looking down, examining my watch, feeling incredibly embarrassed about my unkind behaviour and wishing I could turn back the hands on its face to literally rewind Time and relive it again; only this time, politely and properly.

An hour later, the driver pulled off the road, took a short track up to an open air café and parked under some shady trees. He switched off the engine, got out and walked up to the counter, leaving me sitting there. At first I hesitated but then left the car, expecting to enter the sweltering heat but was pleasantly surprised as, sheltered from harsh sunlight, the air was indeed, unquestionably, more tolerable.

The driver carried two tall glasses over to a small table and sat down. Reluctantly, I joined him. He pushed one of the glasses towards me, picking up the other and drinking it all in one gigantic glug. There followed at least five minutes of silence.

"You dribble when you sleep."

"I beg your pardon?"

"You dribble when you sleep."

I was furious. How dare this Tour Guide, with the ridiculous name, deem to know what I do when I sleep?

"How the Einstein do you know what I do in my sleep?"

"And you snore."

"I do not!"

"You do."

"I most definitely do not snore!"

"You do."

I was livid.

"How dare you come into my bedroom? How dare you walk into my

Daddy's Apartment? Who do you think you are? I'll have you arrested. Take me back: NOW!" I screamed.

"No, I have a commission to show you some outstanding places in this country of mine," he replied as calm as cotton, "and I am not letting your father down, even if you want to!"

I picked up my glass and hurled its contents down the front of his immaculate white shirt, making it cling to the contours of his pleasingly toned, muscular, chest. This unexpected confrontation momentarily took me aback; however, I quickly averted my wide eyes and set off to return to the apartment. Never again did I wish to be in his company, no matter how enthralling his gorgeous body and handsome face might be. I was glad I had been horrid and laughed at his silly name! I walked along the track, out of the protection of the trees and instantly the heat began to seep through my light clothes on to my fair skin. I decided to cut across the scrubland to reach the road. As I stepped into the long, rough grass, I was swept off my feet and thrown, like a sack of yams, over Spring's shoulder: where, despite my struggling and protestations, he quickly took me back to the car, flung me on the back seat and slammed the door.

This was war!

Realising I wouldn't ever be able to compete with his strength, physically, the thought of emotional warfare really appealed to me: thence commenced The Silence. The following few weeks, I remained non-communicative, despite his disturbing presence; displaying no interest whatsoever in anything he said or showed me during our visits to the Zoo, the Monkey Sanctuary, the Botanical Gardens or the many, crowded, bustling markets.

I daren't tell my father; I didn't want to divert him from his important work at the Dam. During one evening meal Daddy asked me if there was anything special I would like to see. I chose a real mud-hut village. Consequently at four, the next morning, I was awoken and told we were travelling up into the Ashanti Region. For this trip, Spring drove a Land Rover; the real, rugged, working model, not the exhibition edition we see on display today.

Radio Silence was still maintained.

The darkness and mist soon gave way to morning light as the main road gave way to untarred tracks, complete with fallen trees and potholes. We pulled into a deserted village; I was mesmerised. The round mud-huts had pointed, straw roofs and stood in circles around a central meeting place. From nowhere, people, wearing very little, appeared and surrounded us. Contrary to Spring's order not to leave the Land Rover, stupidly, I stepped out: a foolish move I will always regret. Immediately, I was engulfed in bodies and felt hands all over my arms, hair and face. Although terrified, I didn't panic or look to Spring for help; he was deep in conversation with a young man, anyway. Suddenly, the crowd parted and a very elderly, white-haired gentleman stood there, shrouded in vibrantly colourful, hand woven Kente cloth and guarded by fearsome warriors, wielding long spears. Aided by a thick, knobbled walking stick, he hobbled up to me, grinning and exposing lots of gum and very little teeth. He then let forth a barrage of words, of which I had absolutely no comprehension.

What was I to do? I am three-quarters British, so I did what we do best: I smiled, nodded and shook his hand, very firmly, saying,

"How do you do? Delighted to meet you."

Instantly, the man let out a whoop of joy and leapt about like a happy frog, throwing his stick in the air and catching it. Everyone joined in his exuberance, singing and dancing as only Africans can.

"Get in the Land Rover, Libby!" Spring bawled across the hullabaloo.

I ignored him.

"Libby, get in the Land Rover!" Spring screamed.

Within moments, I was whisked up in the air and dumped into the back of the Land Rover. Seconds later, Spring jumped into the driver's seat, weaved his way through the throng and sped off, bumping up and down in the numerous potholes on the track. Soon there were shouting and noise and spears whistling past our vehicle. I thought I must be in some Feature Film; this couldn't be real. Spring didn't utter a word; he just looked intently at the road ahead and drove like billy-o.

Once we reached the main road, Spring stopped in a small clearing under some luxuriant trees. He switched off the engine, leant forward, resting his head on the steering wheel and let out a hefty sigh. When he had recovered enough, he took out a hamper from the back of the Land Rover, along with a chunky waterproofed blanket, which he spread on the ground. He opened the hamper and, still standing, we shared some luscious, fresh pawpaw, pineapple and water.

"Spring," I said, realising this was the first civil word I had actually spoken to him, "what happened in the village?"

It took him a while to reply.

"The old man, you know, the one with the walking stick, he was the Village Chief: you must have noticed his clothes were different."

"Yes, he was wearing some."

For the first time I saw a smile on his incredibly beautiful face.

"You Silly, Silly Girl, The Chief asked you to be his twenty-sixth wife and you sealed the deal by shaking his hand!"

"What?" I was horrified. "I was only being polite!"

"Hmmmmmm," he sighed deeply, really deeply, almost painfully, "if only it were as simple as that. This is Africa; you don't break bonds without consequences."

"Spring, I am so sorry," I was genuinely repentant and walked over to a tree and leant up against its sturdy trunk. I lowered my head. "I really am truly sorry….for everything. I am simply a stupid, spoilt, ill-mannered, nearly-a-student! "

He laughed again then followed me over to the tree.

"Libby, I thought I was going to lose you," he whispered, sounding so earnest. He lifted up my head and gently brushed some of my straying hair from off my face.

Suddenly, seeing this magnificent man behaving so tenderly, caught me way off guard, so that when he leaned further in, cupped my face in his hands and kissed me, so softly on my mouth, I melted, responding eagerly. Feeling his body pressed up against mine was ecstasy: the thrill of those incredible kisses, even now, is beyond words.

He pulled away a little and whispered,

"What am I going to do with this, stupid, spoilt, ill-mannered, nearly-a-student?"

"I am sure you have the ability and expertise to train me," I said seriously, "you will have to be prepared to put in a great deal of work to bring me up to standard, though: a great deal of work!"

"Work? What kind of work?"

"Well, to start with, an incredible amount of time will have to be spent on kissing, a really incredible amount of time. 'Are you up to it?' I ask myself."

"I can but try," he whispered, "I think I had better make a start right now though. What do you think?"

I was ecstatic!

The following weeks we lived in Blissville, hardly bearing to be out of each other's air. He took me along rivers and in National Parks; we saw crocodiles, baboons, lions, leopards, elephants, monkeys, porcupines and snakes. He glowed as he showed me his beloved country.

We both declared our love for each other, deciding, although we yearned to be One, we would wait until our wedding night.

My father, who really loved and admired Spring, broke out into raptures! He really couldn't have been more delighted.

Two months later, arriving back at the apartment, after yet another amazing trip, a large, shiny, black Mercedes was parked, flying Diplomatic flags on its polished bonnet.

Spring looked aghast. Four men in immaculate black suits and wearing mirrored sun-glasses, emerged from the car and approached him. Angry shouts were exchanged.

"Libby!" Spring yelled desperately, turning and looking at me as he was man-handled and bundled into the back of the car. Then came the sound of four doors slamming, followed by the screeching of tyres as the car revved round in a half-circle and sped off.

In seconds he was gone: only a rusty-coloured sand cloud and silence remained.

I never, ever saw him again.

I was inconsolable. My father was devastated and did everything possible to comfort me.

We then learnt all about Spring and all about Spring was very much indeed! He was an eminent Zoologist, educated at Eton and then Cambridge University, England and he had won several distinguished International Awards for his work on the conservation of wild life in connection with the forming of the Akosombo Dam. He had unselfishly moved out of his luxurious apartment and given up his Mercedes and Land Rover just for us. What was more, he was an African Prince!

Endless enquiries, searches and investigations were made. The F.B.I. and Interpol were summoned, both trying to discover Spring's whereabouts but despite the expertise of these Government Agencies, he had simply vanished from the curve of the earth.

I returned to England, heartbroken; writing to him every day. A year passed with no response. Finally, I gave up, fearing the worst and started my Degree at Oxford.

Over two years later, my father telephoned to say a letter from Ghana had arrived. He asked me if I wanted him to open it and read it to me.

I declined but asked him to forward it to me in Oxford.

Two days later the letter arrived. However, the following week, I returned home for the Winter Holidays with the letter still unopened and burning a hole in my heart. I was simply too scared to open it without my father, who was bursting to know what had happened.

In the familiar surroundings of my lovely bedroom, I cautiously took the letter out of my bag and gently opened the envelope. Although alone, I was very conscious of my anxious, doting parents awaiting the news, downstairs. The words were beautifully handwritten.

Darling Libby,

How can I write to you after all this time, when I know I have hurt you so much? I didn't want you to feel any blame for what has happened and I hope that by now your heart will have recovered and you will be enjoying a wonderful life at Oxford (oh, and why wasn't it Cambridge)?

Remember the little village we drove to, where the Chief asked you to be his wife? I never told you but my father is Chief of a village twenty five miles further into the Bush. Warriors arrived from the village we visited and approached my father and demanded that he hand you over to be the Bride of the Chief or they would declare war. The young man I was talking to was from my village and when we sped off, he was taken captive. Tribal War is cruel and vicious, Libby, and people are slaughtered.

My father sent messages for me to return you to the Chief but of course, I ignored them.

The only way Tribal War could be avoided was if I agreed to marry the youngest and only unmarried daughter of the Chief, to whom you were betrothed. I had no choice.

Your father told me how much he scorned King Edward V111's decision when he abdicated, choosing his love for Mrs. Simpson over his duty to his country. 'Duty before happiness', he always said.

I hope he honours my painful course.

My heart aches for you, to hold you, to touch you and hear your voice again but I know that will never be.

I am so sorry that I have caused you such pain and I hope you will forgive me?

I will always love you, My Beautiful English Girl,

Spring

P.S. I have written to you many times over the last two years, and never received a reply but I have only just found out that my father saw to it that none of the letters got to you. I know it probably doesn't, but I hope that eases your distress a little to know what anguish that has caused me! My love, ALWAYS, Libby, S.

I wasn't quite expecting my Father's reaction after he had read Spring's letter. Much to my dismay, he threw it violently on the floor.

"'**Never mind your happiness; do your duty**'? What Tosh! Stupid statement! Damn Duty! Damn Druker! What was the man thinking?" he bellowed and stormed out.

I had never heard him raise his voice in my life, ever.

THE END

15

The Face

(I wrote this when people kept telling me how well I was doing, coping with my husband's fatal accident. How little they knew! I wrote the lines in a similar metre to one of my favourite childhood poems, **The Twins** by **Henry Sambrooke Leigh).**

The face she's wearing on my face

Is not my face at all.

The girl that's breathing in this girl

Is really just a wall.

The girl that's 'me', the face you see,

Is just a happy mask.

The breath you hear, the smile I wear,

'Is whose then?' Do you ask?

The one you see, the girl that's 'me'

Is always full of fun.

She laughs a lot, has always got

A smile for everyone.

Within the smile, once in a while,

You'll catch a sudden stare,

As from the 'fun', she longs to run
To someone who could care.

Beneath the face, there lurks a place
Of shadows, pain and sadness.
Under the laugh, there runs a path
Of shudders, blame and badness.

It's not her fault, she'd like to halt
The life she's forced to lead.
Who could she tell about her 'Hell'?
There's no one there who'd heed.

She hoped one day, t'would go away
And leave her safe and free.
Then in its place, would be my face,
Myself I'd truly be.

The face I'd wear upon my face,
Would be my face, you see.
The girl that breathed within this girl
Would really just be me.

THE END

My favourite photograph of my beloved husband with me (taken by Rebekah when she was about eleven)! I miss him indescribably.

I hope you have enjoyed this collection of reflections on my life (apart from Anne's). I really enjoyed compiling them for you!

Carine King

9th March 2015
(If you so wish, you can contact me via www.joni-pip.com)

Lightning Source UK Ltd.
Milton Keynes UK
UKOW07f0656160916

283066UK00014B/85/P